The breathing got louder and louder and louder, huffing into panting, panting into roaring, until she had to clap her hands over her ears to drown it out. Vaz grabbed one of her wrists and dragged her out the back door to the deck, slamming the door shut with his foot.

"Oh, man," he said, shaking his head. "You got ghosts."

Lily's Ghosts

Lily's Ghosts

LAURA RUBY

📚 HARPERTROPHY®
An Imprint of HarperCollinsPublishers

Harper Trophy® is a registered trademark of
HarperCollins Publishers Inc.

Lily's Ghosts
Copyright © 2003 by Laura Ruby
Printed in the United States of America.
For information address HarperCollins Children's Books,
a division of HarperCollins Publishers, 1350 Avenue of the Americas,
New York, NY 10019.

Library of Congress Cataloging-in-Publication Data
Ruby, Laura.
    Lily's ghosts / Laura Ruby.
    p. cm.
    Summary: Strange goings-on at her great-uncle's summer home in Cape
May, New Jersey, draw Lily and a new friend into a mystery involving lost
treasure, a fake medium, and ghosts of all sizes, shapes, and dispositions.
    ISBN 0-06-051829-4 — ISBN 0-06-051830-8 (lib. bdg.)
    ISBN 0-06-051831-6 (pbk.)
    [1.   Ghosts—Fiction. 2.   Mothers   and   daughters—Fiction.
3. Interpersonal relations—Fiction. 4. Cape May (N.J.)—Fiction.] I. Title.
PZ7.R83138Li 2003   2002154315
[Fic]—dc21   CIP
                                                             AC

Typography by Karin Paprocki
❖
First Harper Trophy edition, 2004
Visit us on the World Wide Web!
www.harperchildrens.com

To Melissa and Jessica,
for helping me remember.
And to Steve, for everything.

Acknowledgments

I'd like to thank the good people of Cape May, who let me toy with their history and geography to suit my story. Laura Blake Peterson for sticking it out, Clarissa Hutton for signing me on, Kristin Marang for stepping in, and Janet Frick for checking up. My amazing writer's group: Gina Frangello, Zoe Zolbrod, and Cecelia Downs. Gretchen Moran Laskas, author, confidant, counselor, queen. Tracey George, dear friend, and Melissa Ruby Horan, dear sister, my biggest cheerleaders. Linda Rasmussen for listening to me talk about characters as if they were real people and not once suggesting medication. Annika Cioffi, who gave me "nines"—but only when I earned them. Jennifer Holan and Lynn Voedisch, for the company and the conversation. Katy McGeehee, reader extraordinaire. The incomparable Andrea "Coco" Ohrenich, and all the Ohrenichs, for letting me stay in their lovely house and then letting me make stuff up about it. My parents, Joan Ruby and Richard Ruby, and my in-laws, Fran and Ray Metro, for putting up with my general preoccupation and occasional gloominess. And Stephen Metro, who brought me coffee, baked me cookies, and stole my heart.

BOO Loo BOO Loo BOO Loo BOO Loo BOO Loo BOO Loo BOO Loo BOO Loo BOO

Boo

t he historic city of Cape May, a charming shore village on the tiptoe of New Jersey, is famous for three things: Victorian homes frosted pink and white as the sweetest cakes, sun-washed beaches littered with "diamonds," and many befuddled ghosts.

Most do not know that they are ghosts. They go about their business, bound for the shore or for their old jobs as tour guides or bank tellers or taffy pullers, yammering peevishly at the living. Sometimes they wander the halls of their grand old houses, wondering why guests bring so much furniture and seem to stay for so long.

And then there are those tragic few who understand that their lives have taken an abrupt and brutal turn and that they are helpless to change it. These are the sad ones, the angry ones, the ones who rattle the pipes and steal the socks and hide the house keys in the fridge. These are the ones who scuttle under the beds and whisper *shush, shush* in the dark.

Of course, not everyone who dies becomes a ghost; some souls linger on in this strange twilight while others burst like soap bubbles in the sun, atoms scattering happily, gratefully to the heavens.

Who knows what weighs these sad souls to this earth?
Who knows what haunts the ghosts?

1

Chapter 1

J ust after six in the evening, with the January sky glowering through the windows like a new bruise, Lily decided to throw Uncle Max in the closet.

It wasn't her painting. It wasn't even her house.

But it was a terrible picture. Even her mother thought so, and he was her mother's uncle.

"Oh, that awful thing," her mother had said. "Just ignore it. Don't even look at it."

"How can you *not* look at it?" In the portrait, Uncle Max was just a little older than Lily, but his color was odd and gray and faded, as if he'd spent some time in a washing machine. Pinkish lips flashed a thin zipper of teeth, like the wolf in "Little Red Riding Hood." The eyes, though— the eyes were the worst. Lily thought that if she turned off the lights, the eyes would green up the dark, twirl like pinwheels in the sockets.

"If I looked like that, there's no way I'd let anyone paint a picture of me."

Lily's mother waved her hand. "What does he care? He's dead."

For Lily, it was bad enough that she and her mother had been kicked out of the big white house in Montclair, New Jersey, just that morning. It was bad enough that they had to call Uncle Wesley—whom Lily's mother hadn't seen in years and who was the only family they had left—and beg for a place to stay. And it was bad enough that Lily had to endure four hours on a cramped and wheezing bus with everything she owned stuffed into duffel bags while her cat, Julep, howled like a zoo monkey the whole way.

She was not going to spend the next few months in this strange old house staring at some goggle-eyed, fish-faced dead boy.

She settled on an empty closet in the hall just past the huge staircase. She set the frame on the closet floor, leaning the painting face first against the wall.

"Good night, Uncle Max," she said, and slammed the door shut.

She did not feel any better.

Lily shoved her hands into her pockets and stalked into the living room, or the *parlor*, as her mother had called it. She couldn't help but notice how pretty the room was—all high ceilings and polished floors, antique chairs with their whimsical animal feet—like the summer home of some duchess. But pretty, Lily thought, was deceiving. Pretty meant "Look but don't touch." Pretty meant "Mine but not yours."

The front door belched a cranky moan, and her mother's exasperated voice rang out. "Lord, Lily! You didn't even bring the suitcases upstairs yet!"

"I was looking around."

"It's nice, don't you think?"

Lily shrugged. "If you like museums."

"Oh, well, don't you worry about me," her mother said.

"I'll just lug these four-hundred-pound grocery bags all by myself."

Lily helped carry the bags into the kitchen and empty the contents onto the counter. "Where's the milk?"

Her mother pressed her palms to her temples. "It's official. I'm senile."

"You can always wait until tomorrow morning."

"I need it for my coffee. You know how I get if I don't have my coffee." Lily's mother tossed into the refrigerator the items she had bought. "I won't bother taking off my coat. You wouldn't believe how cold it is out there."

Lily scowled at her mother's orange cape and the loud patchwork skirt peeking out from beneath it. "It's January, Mom. It's supposed to be cold, isn't it?"

"I just didn't think it would be this cold."

"You never think it will be *this* cold," Lily said. *Or this bad or this hard or this long.*

"What are you talking about?"

"Never mind."

Her mother wandered into the dining room, and Lily followed. "Did I tell you that the house has been in the family for more than a hundred years?"

"You told me." Lily took in the china cabinet with its bellyful of crystal, the chandelier that glittered like a small universe over the table. "If this is a summer house, what's the winter house look like?"

"Bigger. More expensive, shiny stuff. We haven't been there in years."

"Was Dad with us?"

If her mother didn't want to answer a question, she did

one of three things: smiled, shrugged, or pursed her lips as if she were blowing a kiss. Her mother smiled her "no comment" smile.

Lily sighed. "So is your uncle Wesley a millionaire or something?"

"Or something," her mother said, laughing. She ran her hand across the surface of the table, the bracelets she had designed herself jangling on her thin arm. "I don't think Uncle Wes has changed anything here since you were little." She smiled. "And it's been a long time since you were little."

Lily inspected the split ends of her long, cinnamon-stick hair. She was used to being as tall as her mother, as tall as an adult. She was thirteen, but sometimes Lily felt like an adult, the way she imagined an adult would feel. Tired. Disappointed.

Her mother sighed. "I can see antiques are not our thing. Did you check if we have cable?" She marched down the hallway past the stairs and into the TV room, Lily trailing behind.

Her mother plucked the remote off the top of the TV and flicked on the machine. "More channels than a teenager could hope for," she said. She looked past Lily to the wall. "Lily? Where's the painting?"

"What painting?" Lily made her own eyes big and round, batting her eyelashes.

"Uh-huh. So innocent. You know what painting." Her mother pointed to the empty space over the mantle.

"Oh, *that* painting. I put it in the closet."

"Lily!"

"It's bad. You said so yourself."

"But I didn't say that you could take it down!"

"Nothing's going to happen to it."

Her mother turned off the TV, sighed at the unadorned wall. "I suppose the closet won't hurt it."

"That's what I thought," Lily said.

Her mother looked from the wall to Lily, Lily to the wall, her expression morphing into her sad clown face, her I'm-sorry face. Lily hoped her mother wouldn't try to hug her.

But instead of reaching for Lily, her mother hid her hands in the voluminous folds of the orange cloak. "I promise that this is going to be okay, okay?"

Lily nodded, thinking that she had once heard a bird with a call just like that, a polite bird that asked, "Okay? Okay? Is it okay if I eat this birdseed? Is it okay if I poop on your head?"

A thin, faraway mewl caught her mother's attention, and she pulled her hands out from the folds in the cloak, smoothed her hair from her face. "You can't keep the cat in that box forever. We'll be here till June, at least. Then we'll get our own place. Maybe even on the beach. How does that sound?"

It sounded like another one of her mother's fantasies, but it was no use telling her. In the dining room, Lily and her mother found Julep looking small and doomed in her cat carrier. Lily opened the latch, and the Siamese stepped out, blinking her blue eyes, poking the air with her wise nose.

Lily stroked the cat's silky fur, but Julep did not press her head into the curve of Lily's palm the way she always did. The cat stared at the ceiling.

"What's up there, Julep?"

Julep vaulted onto one of the chairs and then onto the table. She padded to the middle of the table and sat beneath the chandelier.

Lily's mother leaned a shoulder against the doorjamb. "What's she doing?"

"I don't know."

Julep made a strange sound in her throat, a cross between a meow and moan. She rose up on her hind legs and batted at something with a front paw.

"Oh, *that's* not too creepy," said her mother. "Yikes."

"Maybe there's a spider," Lily said, though she didn't see any spiders. She scratched at the back of her own neck, where the tiny hairs prickled.

"I can't even watch." Lily's mother grabbed the cat. "She shouldn't be on the table anyway," she said, and tossed her to the floor. Julep turned and skidded out of the dining room, down the hallway, and out of sight.

Lily looked up at the chandelier. The crystals winked.

"She's just a little skittish. We're all a little skittish." Her mother clasped both hands over her head and stretched. "I'll be right back with the milk," she said, and strode down the hall toward the front door. When she reached the staircase, she turned. "You know, it smells exactly the same. Like lemon. And tea with mint." She glanced up the staircase as if she expected someone to appear at the top.

"Mom?"

Her mother turned. "Yeah?"

"How did your uncle Max die?"

She made her kissy face. "Why don't you go upstairs

and pick a bedroom? I'll be fifteen minutes, tops."

Lily watched as the door swung shut, then grabbed as many bags as she could carry and dragged them to the second floor. All of the bedrooms were decorated with jumbles of fussy-looking furniture; Lily chose one for herself by putting her duffels on the floor by the closet. She didn't bother to unpack.

She sat on the musty bed, hands knotted on her lap. At the house in Montclair, in the corner of her yellow bedroom, there was a microscope that she'd had to leave behind, a microscope that her mother's boyfriend, the Computer Geek, had bought Lily for her birthday. Lily loved to look at things under it: an eyelash, a bit of dust, a mosquito. She unclasped her hands and rubbed the velvet bedcover. Her microscope was gone. Her friends were gone. The yellow room in Montclair, gone.

Lily felt the tears welling up in her eyes and she swiped at them, squinting them away. She could hear the wind wailing outside, high and thin and human: *Help meeee! Help meeee!* She could smell the faint tang of lemon and tea with mint. She could see Julep crouched beneath the dresser, eyes fluorescent with fear. When the phone rang, Lily pounced on it, realizing after she gulped her eager hellos that there was no one there.

monade LEMONADE lemonade LEMONADE lemonade LEMONADE lemonad

Lemonade

he balding man with the jelly belly and toothpick legs half
sat, half fell on his wife.

"Hey!" said the woman. She, as always, wore a polka-
dotted swimsuit and a bathing cap blooming with bright and
unsettling rubber flowers. "You're crushing me."

"How about making some room, then, instead of hogging the
whole sheet?"

The wife rolled her eyes and moved two inches to the left.
Husband and wife watched the gray sea curl and unfurl like a
tongue. If they did not seem bothered by the frigid winter air, it
was because they couldn't feel it.

"Did you bring the lemonade?" the man said.

"No," said the woman. "I thought you brought the lemonade."

The man shook his head. "Didn't I ask you to bring the lemonade before we got into the car?"

"Where *is* the car?" asked the woman.

"Where we left it."

"Oh." The woman fluffed the big floppy flowers on her
bathing cap. "Where *did* we leave it?"

The man frowned at his wife. "I don't know. All I know is that
I want some lemonade."

The two had left their car in a ditch twenty-three years before,
after the man swerved to avoid some geese crossing the road.

11

"Should we see if the concession stand is open yet?"

"Forget it. Let's just go swimming before the crowds get here."

The woman laughed, pointed at the ocean, where numerous heads bobbed in the icy surf. "We're too late."

"Darned kids," the man said. They watched as one of them, a girl of about thirteen or fourteen, ran out of the water. She was wearing a woolen dress over pantaloons. "Where do they get those crazy outfits?"

"At least she's not walking around half naked like some of the other ones," said the wife, throwing a stern look at another teenager prancing around the beach in a black leotard, fishnet stockings, and a tiny satin skirt. "But that wool dress looks awfully heavy."

The girl, who had drowned in 1909, was running up and down the beach in the sodden dress calling, "Father! Father? Where are you? Father?"

The woman's brows furrowed in worry. "Do you think she's lost?"

"Looks like," said the man.

"Do you think we should help her?"

"She'll be fine."

The woman harrumphed. It was one of her favorite things to do.

"Get a load of that guy," said her husband, shaking his head at a caped figure wearing knee breeches and a plumed hat.

The woman gestured to a tall fellow in animal-skin pants, shells, and feathers making his way down the beach toward them. "And what do you think *he's* dressed up for?"

"Lunatics," the man said. "I don't know why they don't lock up all these people where they belong."

The man, a Lenape Indian who had died in a skirmish with

Dutch settlers in 1644, stopped suddenly and gaped at the man and his wife before hurrying off in the opposite direction, his moccasins kicking up sand in stiff sprays as he ran.

"Well! What spooked him?" asked the woman, indignant.

The man looked at his wife's bathing cap, at the rubber flowers sprouting from it like Brussels sprouts. "Beats me."

Chapter 2

The house—shiny and drapey and mossy with doilies—loomed so huge and imposing that for the first week Lily felt like a hamster scratching around in it. And she kept touching things, things she knew she shouldn't. She wondered how she was going to make herself at home, even for a little while, when she had to keep rubbing her fingerprints off everything.

At least there's no boyfriend this time, she consoled herself. Except for the distant uncle in Philadelphia, and the dead one in the closet, Lily and her mother were pretty much on their own.

It wouldn't stay that way for long.

Here's how it always happened: Lily's mother, Arden, met a man. Arden and the man would date. Soon they would make plans. Plans to move. Plans to get married. Plans to start a business. They planned and planned and planned until the plans were so elaborate that the man would get all tangled up in them, forget his part. Finally the man, whoever he was, would announce he needed his "space" and would shuffle away, shaking his head like a cat who'd landed on his feet after a dizzying fall.

Lily knew all this because she was there, sitting at the restaurants or in the movie theaters, playing with her straw wrappers as her mother and the men cooked up their schemes. The men would try to ask Lily questions when they noticed her.

"And what do you like to do?" They asked this because Lily's mother was an artist and they assumed Lily was one, too.

"Science experiments," Lily might answer.

Lily's mother explained, "Lily's a bit more practical."

And because the men were mostly practical, and mostly terrified that they would be practical for the rest of their lives, their faces would fill with a mixture of pity and disgust, as if her mother had said, "Lily has head lice."

The men had no names. Lily referred to them by their occupations: Dental Man, Insurance Boy, Gear Head, and that traitor, Computer Geek. Lily wondered what her mother would scare up next. Grocery Guy? Fish Guts?

Clutching a pile of books, Lily eased into one of the high-backed chairs in the parlor. It might have been worth a fortune, but it was about as comfy as a pile of rocks. She moved into the dining room to try the chairs there.

In the window facing her, a shadow flickered, stopping Lily in her tracks. A rubbery-looking white hand popped up and pressed into the glass like a starfish, the fingers stiff as tiny periscopes. Her eyelids shuddered in surprise, and then the hand was gone.

Her mother swept down the hall and into the room. "Morning!" she sang. Her eyes followed Lily's startled gaze, and she raised her eyebrows.

"There was a hand in the window," said Lily, pointing. "Somebody's hand, reaching up against the glass outside."

Her mother shrugged. "Maybe someone was waving at you. This is a small town. People are friendly."

"What people? Nobody knows we're here."

"Except for the man next door," said her mother.

They had gotten the house keys from the neighbor, as Uncle Wesley had told them to. Not much taller than Lily, with a wobbly head and a wormy body, their neighbor looked like a giant baby in a bad mood. Angry Baby Man.

Lily dropped her books on the dining-room table. "What kind of person just goes around slapping their greasy hands on people's windows?"

"There are only a few thousand year-round residents in Cape May." Her mother tapped the pile of books. "And I'm sure that most of them and their hands are in school right now."

"Uh-huh," Lily said. She was sure the year-round residents, if there were any, were all shut up in their restored Victorians, polishing their antiques and counting their money. Or maybe they all had maids for that kind of thing.

Lily's mother rummaged in her coat pockets, in her purse. "Did you see the house keys? I thought I put them in my pocket." Lily's mother paused in her search. "You can still change your mind about school, you know."

Lily watched the window for another hand or maybe a foot or an elbow. "You said I wouldn't have to change schools again. You promised you would homeschool me, Mom."

Her mother chewed her lip. "Yes, but how are you going to make any friends?"

Lily thought of Wendy, her best friend in kindergarten,

Susan in fourth grade. Karen from Montclair. Saying good-bye to them all. "I'll join the local football team."

"I'm sure the kids here are very nice."

"So I make friends with the nice kids and then we move to Kentucky or France or somewhere."

"Why would we ever move to Kentucky?"

"We've moved everywhere else."

Her mother threw up her hands. "Okay, okay. But just until the end of the year. It's high school in September for you." Arden pulled her bushy hair away from her face and snapped a rubber band around it. Two blond curls sprang free and stuck out like antennae. "And now I have to go to work."

"You said the store doesn't open up until March."

"It doesn't, but I have a lot of planning and cleaning to do. Uncle Wesley had to pull a few strings to get me the assistant manager's position, and the owners are taking his word for it that they can trust me to run it by myself until the summer season begins. I want to get a head start." She jingled her bracelets. "Besides, I'm going to make some more just like these, maybe with shells. Something beachy. What do you think?"

Lily imagined her mother spending what little money they had left on silver and garnets and paper clips just so that she could make some of her strange earrings shaped like toasters. Or since they were now living at the beach, lobsters. Lobsters on toast.

Her mother grabbed the pencil out of Lily's hand and scribbled a telephone number in Lily's notebook. "Here's the number for the store, just in case." Arden looked down at the stacks of books. "Homeschooling, huh? Am I crazy or what?" she said to the cat, who sat on one of the dining-room chairs gazing placidly at the ceiling.

Lily pointed. "What do you think she sees up there?"

"She's a lovely little thing, but she has a brain the size of a fig." Her mother turned out her pockets. "And so do I, apparently."

"Just go, Mom. I'll look for the keys later. I'm sure they're around somewhere."

"Okay." Her mother slipped on her orange cloak. "I'll be home around noon. I want you to strip the beds and put the sheets and towels in the wash."

"Mom!"

"*And* I want one chapter in that math book finished."

"Mom!"

"You were the one who wanted to be homeschooled. I'm not a total pushover."

Lily waited until she heard the front door close before she got up and went to the window. She craned her neck in both directions, but there was nothing to see. No shadows, no rubbery hands, not even a squirrel dancing along the sill. It was as if the entire world were fast asleep.

Lily finished her math chapter in a couple of hours, stripped the beds, and then dragged all the laundry to the basement. She had expected something dark and dank, but the room was crosshatched by bright yellow sunbeams that shot through the small high windows. There wasn't much: more fussy furniture; a stack of boxes; a washer and dryer; her mom's old Kewpie doll sitting in a chair, its little hands like fat pink stars against its bright red dress.

The Kewpie was one of the few things Lily's mom insisted on dragging from place to place. "My mother left it to me," she'd say. "I can't get rid of it," though she always stashed it somewhere no one would see it.

Lily separated the whites from the colors and stuffed the sheets and towels into the machine, using dish soap for laundry detergent. After flipping on the washer, she kicked the rest of the wash into a pile by the boxes.

It couldn't hurt to take a peek into them, she thought, walking over to lift the lid of the closest one. An old desk lamp, a radio, some other junk. She pushed the box aside to get to the next box, a lot heavier than the first. *National Geographics*, some old, some more recent, almost all with the ocean on the cover.

She knelt on the floor and flipped through the magazines, looking for pictures of sharks and squid and weird-looking fish. There were photos of the Great Barrier Reef in Australia (pretty cool), poison jellyfish (very cool), and an article about finding the *Titanic* in the Atlantic. Robert Ballard, the guy who found the *Titanic*, talked about how he didn't find any skeletons in the wreck because bones dissolve quickly in the deep ocean, that the only thing left of the passengers was their shoes; the sea animals didn't know enough to eat the leather.

Lily looked up from the article, imagining rows and rows of shoes, their laces dancing sadly in the purple murk of the ocean. The Kewpie watched from its perch, its chubby arms splayed in a plastic imitation of bouncing baby joy.

Lily frowned. Weren't the arms *down* before?

She stared, unblinking. The doll's bald head—anointed with a single blond curl on the crown—was cast downward, but its huge, round eyes peeked out sideways from under the lashes, as if it had just noticed her, as if it were amused. Lily gave the doll a hesitant half wave before she realized what she was doing and then, feeling tremendously stupid, dropped her hand.

Rolling her eyes at herself, Lily went back to the *Titanic* article. What was interesting was that this guy Ballard didn't try to collect any of the shoes, though even soggy old oxfords from the *Titanic* would be worth a ton of money. He felt that the shoes marked a special place and that disturbing them would be wrong. Too many people, the article said, looked at shipwrecks as just another way to get rich rather than a way to learn about ourselves. People thought more of money than they did of history or of science.

At this, Lily snorted. She thought plenty of science, but how many millions of dollars had it cost to fund the scientific expedition to *find* the *Titanic*? If there wasn't any money, there wasn't much science.

She tossed the magazine back into the box, glancing at the Kewpie. Now the head faced squarely forward and the black irises, which had peeked so coyly and sweetly out of the corners of its eyes, looked straight at her.

Lily's jaw unhinged like a snake's, her lungs suddenly stripped of oxygen. She closed her eyes, took a deep breath, then opened her eyes again, testing. The doll didn't move. Her breathing slowed. Well, of course it didn't move! It was a *doll*. She was just seeing it from a different angle, that's all.

Lily rubbed her cheeks. First phone calls, then hands,

now dolls. What was wrong with her? Leaving Montclair, that was it. Well, it was no use thinking about that.

She stuck out her tongue at the Kewpie and began packing up the rest of the magazines the way she found them. Lily had been given tons of cheap baby dolls over the years, mostly by her mother's boyfriends. As a little girl, she'd liked to pull off the arms and legs to see how they were attached, liked to pluck out the eyes to see what they were made of.

"I don't like dolls," she said, her voice reverberating off the concrete walls. "No brains. No guts."

A hollow clattering behind her rocked her on her heels, and she wheeled around, gripped the dryer. The Kewpie had somehow tumbled out of the little wooden chair and now sat on the floor, arms up over its head, blunt sausage fingers beseeching. Like it wanted to be picked up. Like it wanted—

"Oh, come on!" Lily hissed at herself. She forced herself to approach the doll. Its dimpled, sickeningly sweet smile seemed like a leer. *Go ahead*, it said. *Pick me up, I dare you. I'll grab you with my sticky baby fingers and I'll . . .*

Lily grabbed it by its cold, plastic throat and shoved it back into a sitting position on the chair. Then she backed away and walked upstairs, willing herself to step slowly through the dining room and hallway, casually up the main staircase, though her stomach clenched and her muscles hummed.

She went into the bathroom and took a brush from the medicine cabinet. "No brains, no guts, no brains, no guts," she muttered as she gave her long hair a dozen painful, vigorous strokes. Even up in the bathroom, Lily could hear the thrum of the washing machine. And then another noise, quieter, sneaking underneath it. She cocked her head and squinted. There it was again, a creaking sound, thin and faint, like a door opening into another world. Then a muted *tap, tap, tap*. Slow and stealthy.

Like footsteps. Like tiny footsteps.

Her eyes flew open wide, the brush sliding out of her hand and into the sink. "Mom?" she said, she hoped.

She left the bathroom and slowly walked down the stairs. The front door was shut. She made her way into the dining room and then into the kitchen. "Mom! Mom?"

No Mom. Lily stood still, listening for the creak, for the footsteps, but now all she heard was the dumb drone of the refrigerator. She checked the back door, but it was bolted from the inside.

Lily walked back to the front door, opened it, and looked out onto the front porch. She turned her head left and right, scanning the street, but saw no one but a lone mailman wearing a crazy blue hat with fuzzy antlers, even though Christmas had come and gone.

She stepped back inside the house and slammed the door shut, trying to erase from her mind the kooky-freaky images of Kewpie dolls hopscotching around the basement.

This is nuts. Hands don't float, dolls don't walk, and life isn't some stupid horror movie. She would put her schoolbooks away and watch some soap operas, and then her mother would come home and things would be normal . . . well, maybe not normal, but familiar.

But her books weren't on the table where she had left them. They were gone. In their place sat Julep, blue eyes blinking, the house keys Lily's mother had lost lying at her tiny brown feet.

The phone rang shrilly, and Lily snatched up the receiver without thinking, without taking her eyes from the keys.

"Hello?" she said.

A deep voice rasped, "Hello, Lily."

Lily dropped the phone, scooped the keys from the dining-room table, and ran out the front door.

She raced into the backyard and all the way around the house, moving so fast that by the time she saw the tall, skinny boy walking down the sidewalk with his head thrown back, paper towels up his nose, she couldn't stop. She crashed right into him, toppling them both.

Whatever
Lola Wants

*L*ola stomped down the sidewalk in her leotard, fuchsia satin skirt, and stocking feet, shaking the sand from her black character shoes and thinking that this whole death thing was totally bogus.

First of all, she had to wear the same outfit every day. Second, there was nothing to do. Third, there was nobody to hang out with.

"You're supposed to *eat* your broccoli," she'd said to the woman in the gag-me bathing cap, "not glue it to your hat."

"I bet your mother doesn't know what you're wearing," said the woman.

"I bet you don't know that you're *dead*."

The woman had clutched at her chest and called Lola a hoodlum. Puh-lease. What did people have against a little friendly conversation?

This was all Steffie's fault, right down to the frump in the bathing cap. If Steffie hadn't stolen the lead in the school musical, then she wouldn't be stuck wearing this stupid satin skirt for all eternity. *She* would have starred as Lola, the sexy satanic seductress in *Damn Yankees*. And *she* would have been the one that the guys were drooling over instead of being some lame sidekick chorus girl no one noticed.

The play was about an old guy who sells his soul to the devil to become a baseball star, but afterward tries to worm out of the deal. The devil sends the lovely Lola to sweeten the offer. Everyone knew that she had that part wrapped up. It was practically written for her! And then Steffie, this plain-as-paper nobody from the science club, shows up at the auditions, wows dorky Mr. Pringle, the director, and ruins everything. The science club! Science geeks can't sing! They don't wear fishnets!

She couldn't even remember how it happened—when, exactly, she died. One minute she was at the cast party, slurping spinach dip and giving Steffie the evil eye; the next she was sprawled on a darkened stage dressed in her stupid sidekick satin skirt, surrounded by ghosts—most of them so dull and oblivious she longed to shoot herself in the head, pointless as *that* would be. She figured that it was something she was born with, a weak heart or broken blood vessel or some sort of majorly rare, impossible-to-detect cancer.

Anyway, her death was tragic, that much she knew. It was always tragic when somebody with her looks and talent and potential was "taken" so young. She had been destined for great-ness. Hadn't her mother said . . . um . . . well, she couldn't remem-ber exactly what her mother had said, or even what her mother looked like, but her mother must have said some wonderful, loving, motherly type things. Her father, too. She wondered if she had any brothers or sisters.

"Whatever Lola wants," she sang. She might be dead, but she still had a killer voice. She *was* Lola. Even if she hadn't forgotten her real name — did it begin with a *B* or maybe a *D*?—she'd call herself Lola just to prove how totally Lola she was.

Unlike Steffie the doof, who was just some pathetic geekazoid Lola wanna-be.

Some guy, a live one, was staggering down the sidewalk with something stuck up his nose, gross! But Lola plunked herself down in the middle of the walk anyway—what did she care? He'd stagger right through her—and slipped into her shoes. That's when the redhaired girl burst from the Victorian house right in front of her, ran a crazy lap around her house, then barreled right into the guy.

If Lola had possessed a heart, it would have hammered out a mambo beat.

Steffie.

It was Steffie, she was sure of it. But what did that dipstick do to her hair? It was a long scraggly wreck, even worse than before. Hadn't she ever heard of a haircut? A perm? An *exorcist*? And the clothes! Flared jeans! Gag! She looked like a reject from the disco era. Didn't she know it was 1987 already? (Or maybe it was 1988 now; it was kind of hard to keep track.) Anyway, the geek needed some serious help.

She cracked a wide crocodile smile.

Lola was just the girl to help her.

Chapter 3

The boy lay motionless on the grass. "Hey, are you all right?" Lily said. "I'm sorry. I didn't see you."

"Mmmng," the boy mumbled. "Mngirken."

"What?" Lily scrambled over to him, saw the blood freckling the front of his green coat, the paper towels he held to his nose.

He pulled the bloody wad away from his face. "My nose," he honked, "was already broken. And now I think it's sideways, too."

Lily leaned closer to inspect his nose. It wasn't pretty. "It's a little lumpy," she said, "but it's where it's supposed to be."

"Cool. So it only *feels* like it's sideways."

"I said sorry." Lily sat back on her heels. "What happened to you?"

"Darren Sharp happened to me," he said, sitting up. "He happened to want to try out his blue belt or yellow belt or whatever belt in karate. But don't think he's good or anything. My nose is hard to miss." The boy sneezed, then groaned. His enormous brown eyes watered. "So, what happened to you?"

"What do you mean?"

"I don't know. Most people don't run laps around their houses."

"Not like it's your business or anything, but somebody was creeping around my house, moving around my stuff."

"Really?" His battered face perked up, as if he liked the idea of anonymous somebodies creeping around. "Do you have any idea who it was?"

Lily picked at the strands of hair tickling her cheeks and stood up. "I don't know *who* it was. All I know is that there was somebody looking in my window this morning, and then someone came in and stole some things. I thought I could catch him."

"How do you know it's a him?" the guy said.

"Him, her, who cares?" Lily put her hand in her pocket and felt for the house keys. What if the person who had stolen them had already made a copy? Despite the cold, Lily felt a trickle of sweat drift its way down her stomach. "I have to call my mother," she said absently.

"Okay. So where's your mother?"

"At the store."

"Really? Around here? Which store?"

This was one of the reasons Lily hadn't wanted to go to junior high. Too many dumb guys. "Shouldn't you be in school or something?"

"Shouldn't you be?"

"For your information, I *am* in school," she said. She was glad he was still sitting on the ground so that she could tower over him. She glared at the guy, at the deserted street and sidewalk. She hated being afraid.

He struggled to his feet. "Is this your house?"

"No."

"Whose house is it?"

30

"My great-uncle's."

"So maybe it was your great-uncle in the house."

"He's not even in town. He's in Philadelphia."

"That's a cool city." The boy tilted his shaggy head and smiled through the smeared blood. "You're new here, aren't you? Where are you from?"

Even with the broken nose and the blood and the twigs decorating his dark hair, Lily could see how cute he was, and for some reason it irked her even more.

She folded her arms across her chest. "You don't want to know where I'm from."

He rolled his eyes. "Okaaay," he said, drawing the sound out. "Maybe I don't." He lifted his hand, which was smeared with blood. "Look, do you think maybe you have a couple of tissues you can give me, or some paper towels or something?"

"I don't think we have any tissues," Lily said. "*Or* paper towels."

"Yeah, all right, I get the hint. I'm leaving," he said. "I guess I'll see you around. *Or* not."

She watched him turn and stumble away. The back of his jacket was covered with grass stains and black streaks of dirt. She hoped that the stains were from his fight with the Karate Kid, but worried that they weren't. What if he asked her to pay for the cleaning? What if he needed a whole new coat?

"Wait," she said.

He raised his arm without turning around, like a man flagging a taxi. "Don't worry about it."

"No, no," she said. "Wait." He stopped. She pulled her

ratty sweatshirt over her head, careful not to take off her T-shirt with it, and held the raggedy thing out to him. "Here," she said. "It's better than a paper towel." She crossed her bare arms, hugging herself against the bracing wind.

He looked at the shirt, then at her. "I can't take your shirt. I'll get crud all over it. And you'll turn into a Popsicle."

"It's old. I was going to throw it out anyway," she said. "Take it. I'm fine."

"Are you sure?"

"I'm sure." She thrust the sweatshirt at him.

"Thanks," he said.

She watched him press the sweatshirt to his ruined nose, which did look pretty mangled. "I'm sorry I ran into you," she said.

He shrugged. "Yeah, well, I guess if I had some freak lurking around my house, I'd start running around, too." He paused. "Are you sure you saw somebody in your window? Maybe it was a bird or something."

"Yes, I'm sure!" she said. "I don't go around seeing things."

"Peace, okay? I was just asking."

"Besides," Lily said, "whoever it was took all my schoolbooks."

"Why would anyone want to take all your schoolbooks?"

"How should I know?"

"Are you sure you didn't move them or put them somewhere?"

"I think I would have remembered moving my books,"

Lily said, exasperated.

The boy raised a single eyebrow. Lily decided that he was an idiot.

"Well," Lily said. "I hope you can find a doctor to fix your nose."

"Good luck finding your burglar-intruder-whoever." The guy smiled with half his mouth. "But if you find him, why don't you send him to my house? Tell him he can have *my* schoolbooks."

Lily whipped around and marched toward the house, but her foot caught on something and she went sprawling onto the cold, hard ground.

"Are you okay?" the guy said, clearly fighting a laughing fit. He held out his hand to help her up.

She eyed him with suspicion.

"Your shoelace," he said, pointing to one of her sneakers. "Mom always said it was dangerous."

Face burning, she quickly knotted the untied lace. "I'm fine," she said, ignoring his hand and jumping to her feet.

"You don't look—"

"I'm fine, I'm fine." She cut him off, turned, and raced up the porch stairs. She opened the front door and slammed it shut as hard as she could.

Once inside, however, the fear hit her again like a bad smell. She rubbed her face, then her bare arms with her hands, suddenly colder than she had been outside. Who had called the house? Was it the same person who stole the books? How could somebody have gotten inside the house to get the keys in the first place? The person could have been right there in the room with her! But who could he be?

Where could he be?

Eyes wide, she kept as still as she could and listened for any sounds in the house.

And there it was. But different this time. Faster. Bolder. Coming from the parlor.

Lily almost ran back outside to get the guy with her shirt up his nose. But she thought of his one raised eyebrow, the blood like war paint on his cheeks, and steeled herself. She peeked into the parlor.

And found Julep perched on the arm of one of the big, stiff chairs, thwacking the pull chain of a lamp against its wooden base.

"Julep!" she yelled, then groaned. "Now who's the fig brain?"

The cat mewled and kept thwacking, her eyes round Os of kitty glee.

"Glad to see someone's making herself at home." Lily rubbed her forehead with her hand, then knocked on it as if to pound in some sense. Maybe Broken-Nose Boy was right. She must have forgotten about moving the books. She must have brought them upstairs or something. It was possible. More possible than anyone wanting to steal them.

Still knocking on her forehead, she walked up the stairs. Once on the landing, however, she paused. Instead of the warm, lemon-minty scent that usually permeated the house, there was another scent: faint and sooty, like burnt toast. She followed her nose to a staircase partially hidden above the main staircase. A white door with a shiny knob like an eye perched at the top. The attic. She climbed the staircase and tried the knob, but it wouldn't budge, no matter how hard she tugged. Pressing her eye to the key-hole, she tried to see inside, but the opening was too small. The sooty smell was gone, if it had even been there at all.

Lily stomped back down the stairs. *Well, Lily, what's your hypothesis? The Kewpie cooked up some toast for a snack? A book-swiping burglar decided to light himself a campfire in the attic?*

Yeah, right. Old houses made a lot of noise, old houses smelled bad, old houses were weird. She'd have to get used to it. To all of it.

She threw open the door to her bedroom. Piled neatly on the low table next to the bed, Lily found her books.

She also found the Kewpie doll, with its sweet baby eyes and pink crescent grin, sitting on the bed, arms up, waiting.

the good fortunes shoppe THE GOOD FORTUNES SHOPPE the good fortunes s

The Good fortunes Shoppe

Cape May's outdoor mall was a cheerful strip of ice-cream, T-shirt, jewelry, and souvenir shops lining a brick pedestrian walkway. In the summer the walkway teemed with children slurping ice-cream cones, teenagers elbowing and jostling one another, and parents in ill-fitting Bermuda shorts buying hermit crabs and other vacation necessities.

But now it was January, and many of the mall's stores were shut tight for the winter.

Except for Madame Durriken's Good Fortunes Shoppe.

Though it was popular with tourists and townies alike, the town officials weren't too fond of the Shoppe, and had twice held referendums to have it closed down—some for religious reasons, most for reasons of taste. The Good Fortunes Shoppe—stocked with tarot-card decks, candles, astrology charts, incense, dream interpretation books, spell manuals, and a large selection of moon-embroidered satin cloaks—was open year-round to anyone looking for a way to tell the future.

And if you weren't interested in learning to tell your own future, for twenty-five dollars Madame Durriken would do it for you.

Madame Durriken, whose real name was Maple Ann Spatz, was uncommonly tall and gaunt with diaphanous gray hair like dandelion fluff. She read palms and tarot cards and, occasionally, foreheads. She also claimed to be able to see—and speak to—the dead.

Madame Durriken enjoyed her work.

"Let me see," she might say as she traced a crease in a palm, her forehead equally creased in concentration. "You will have a long life, a long, *long* life, and much financial success. But," she would say, raising an eyebrow so high that it was swallowed up by her fluffy gray hair, "you are unlucky in love." She would cluck her tongue in sympathy, stretching the skin on the palm, tipping the hand toward its unsuspecting owner. "See this little break? Right here? This is a *divorce!*"

The sad truth was that Madame Durriken could tell the future about as well as the weathermen; that is to say, not very well at all, and the deceased wouldn't talk to her if she were the last person on earth—living *or* dead.

Madame Durriken's current customer, her only customer on this chilly January morning, was poor Mrs. Wilma Hines, who was hoping to speak to her husband again. She couldn't find the checkbook, and the heating bill needed to be paid. She was sure Mr. Hines, dead for some fourteen years, would know where it had gotten to.

Madame Durriken sighed and led the shuffling Mrs. Hines through a doorway covered with heavy red velvet curtains into the tiny makeshift room where she did all her readings. She yearned for the heat of July and August that thrust the bubble-brained young women into the Shoppe, aching and desperate for some bit of news about rock-headed young men. She loved laying out the tarot cards one by one, her frown deepening with each card. She loved taking the girls' young hands into her own skeletal ones, watching as the girls' excitement wilted like a fresh hairdo in the heat when she said, "You're in some trouble, dear. This boy is up to no good."

But twenty-five dollars was twenty-five dollars, and Madame Durriken wasn't going to turn away money, especially in the winter with business so thin. She sat Mrs. Hines in the folding chair across the glitter-strewn table and took her place in the big armchair against the wall.

"Now, Wilma, you remember what you need to do, don't you?"

"Oh, yes." Wilma hefted a purse the size of a sewing machine onto the table. "I must close my eyes and concentrate."

Madame Durriken reached across the table, plucked up the purse, and set it on the floor. "Not on the table, dear. The spirits don't like clutter."

"Oh, my. I'm sorry," said Mrs. Hines, glancing around. She gazed at the ceiling. "I'm sorry."

"It's quite all right, Wilma." Madame Durriken placed a large candle shaped like a bat in the middle of the table and lit it. "Why don't we get started? Now, you do what you did the last time. Put your hands flat on the table, and you concentrate very hard on Mr. Hines. We'll see if we can't get your husband to join us for a little visit."

Mrs. Hines giggled at the idea of her dead husband joining them for a "little visit." She put her palms flat on the table and closed her eyes. Madame Durriken intoned, "Spirits of the dead, can you hear us? We beseech you! We are calling Harold Hines! Harold? Your dear wife needs to speak with you! Harold! Come to us now!"

Mrs. Hines shivered in anticipation, and Madame Durriken

stifled a yawn. She quietly stood up from her chair and drifted to the window, which was completely covered with black-and-gold draperies. Nudging the draperies aside, she risked a peek to the brick walkway outside. A blond woman wearing an orange cloak and a funky patchwork skirt was standing at the door of the Something Fishy gift shop across the street, muttering to herself as she patted her pockets.

"Harold! We beseech you!" barked Madame Durriken as she wondered who the woman might be and where she might have gotten the snazzy cloak. Philadelphia? New York City?

She was so busy thinking about the cloak, how many she should order and how much she could charge for them, that she almost didn't see the tall boy loping like some sort of ostrich behind the blond woman. And even then—as Madame Durriken took in his peculiar clothes, bluish skin, the queer shine of his eyes—it was a moment before she registered that she could not only see the boy, she could see *through* the boy.

And that he had seen her, too.

The spirit boy grinned right at Maple Ann Spatz and held out his cloudy hands as each one burst into flame.

Chapter 4

"I'm telling you, Mom, someone was in the house. I heard him."

"Lily, I'm sorry, I just don't believe that anyone would break into the house to move your books around." Her mother hung her orange cloak on the coat tree. "What do you think about pancakes for lunch?"

"We had those for dinner last night," said Lily. "And breakfast this morning." She followed her mother down the hallway and into the kitchen. "So what about the doll? How did the doll get from the basement to my bed?"

"Are you sure that you didn't—"

Lily stamped her foot, feeling like a baby as she did it but unable to stop herself. "Why does everyone think that *I* did it?"

"Who's everyone?" Her mother pulled the elastic from her hair, then fluffed the blond curls with her fingers. "And anyway, people forget things all the time. When I used to drive to work, sometimes I couldn't remember a single thing that happened along the way. It was like I had arrived at work in a blink."

"That's not what happened. I didn't move my books. I didn't bring the doll up from the basement. And I didn't forget."

"What about Julep?"

"You think Julep took my math books?"

"No, I think you took your books upstairs and forgot you did it, just like you forgot the keys on the table." Her mother pulled the ham from the drawer in the fridge, along with an old, tattered book. "And I guess the thief must have stashed this in the cheese drawer just to be safe." She smiled at Lily as she tossed the book to the counter. "*The Standard Guide to Rare Coins*? Not your usual fare."

Lily stared at the book. "I don't know how that got in there!"

"Uh-huh," said her mother, unwrapping the ham.

"Maybe the guy put that in there!"

Lily's mother waved her hands, bracelets jangling. "Oh, it was probably in there before and we didn't notice it. Uncle Wes is old. He probably has all kinds of funky stuff all over the place."

Lily nudged the book with a finger. "So what about the doll?"

"What about it?"

"How did the doll get upstairs?"

"Julep."

"What? How?"

"Don't you remember?" Her mother opened the bag of white bread and removed four slices. "She used to pull your socks from the drawers and hide them under the couch?"

"It's not the same," Lily said.

"And what about the time she stole your teddy bear? We were looking all over the house for it, and then she trotted by with it hanging from her mouth. Couldn't she have done the same to the doll?"

"And then she arranged it on my bed?"

Lily's mother slapped some ham onto the bread. "Look, Lily, I don't know how she did it, but I don't see any other explanation." She topped the sandwiches with a second slice of bread. "I know you're angry with me."

Lily pulled out one of the kitchen chairs and sat at the table. "That's not it."

"I know you didn't want to leave Montclair. And I know you don't like the house much. Maybe you hate the house. Maybe you even hate me. But that doesn't mean that there are crazy burglars running around. Besides, we have to make the best of it, all right?" Her mother put the gold-rimmed plates on the table. "Now will you look at this service? What other kid has it so good, hmmm?"

Her mother ate her ham sandwich while Lily ripped hers into a lot of little pieces, rolling them into balls before popping them into her mouth.

"It's a stupid doll," Lily said finally.

Her mother looked hurt. "It was my mother's. And before that it belonged to my grandmother."

Lily was unmoved. "It's stupid. And ugly."

"So maybe we should throw it in the closet with Uncle Max."

"Maybe we should make Julep do it."

Her mother didn't answer. Lily rolled a ham-and-bread ball between her thumb and index finger. She remembered the phone call. "Somebody called, too. Somebody who knew my name. Tell me that's not weird."

Her mother put down the remains of her sandwich. "Oh,

Lily! That was Uncle Wes. He called the store and wanted to know why you hung up on him. I told him that he must have misdialed. He just wanted to know how we were settling in."

"Oh," Lily said, feeling like a bigger fig brain than ever. "What did you say?"

"I told him that we were fine." Lily's mother sighed. "We only spoke for a few minutes. He just wipes me out."

"What do you mean?"

For a minute, Lily thought that her mother wouldn't answer the question, but she said, "Like I told you, he's a strange old guy. I suppose I should feel sorry for him. He lost his father. Then his brother, Max, then his mother, all in a short time. And my mom—his sister—just a few years ago. Still . . ."

"Still?"

"Oh, this is old news," said her mother, shrugging. "Old news is rarely ever good news. Let's just talk about something else."

Lily knew by her mother's shrug that she'd say no more about Uncle Max. "How was work?"

"Work was work," Arden said, getting up and bringing the dishes to the sink. "I didn't have much with me. A few stones. A bit of silver." Lily's mother dropped her head, as if sizing up her feet.

"Did you make anything?"

"Some things," she said. "I was a little distracted." Her mother's eyes were glassy, and Lily was afraid that she might start crying. Lily didn't think she could stand it if her mother started crying again. It made Lily feel helpless, then angry. What had her mother thought? That they

44

would live with the Computer Geek happily ever after?

Lily's mother didn't cry. She turned on the water, rinsed off the china plate, and set it next to the sink. "But then, what's done is done. It's much more fun to think about what's next, right?"

"Right."

Her mother wiped at her eyes. "Something funny did happen, though."

"What?"

"Just as I was about to lock up Something Fishy, this woman, this crazy woman comes running out of the shop across the street, screaming and waving." Her mother pantomimed, pinwheeling her arms. "She looked like a giant dandelion with limbs."

"What was she screaming about?"

"I don't know. Something about a boy who was on fire."

"What's up with that?"

"I have no idea. I didn't have a chance to ask her either. She ran right back into her store. I could see her peeking out at me through the curtains. It was the weirdest thing." She gestured to Lily's plate. "If you're done playing with your food, maybe you want to go out and take a walk or something. It's not that cold."

"But, Mom!"

"Come on, Lily. Give it a chance? For me? It's a great little town. And who knows? Maybe you'll run into somebody interesting."

Lily tucked her hands into her pockets and breathed deeply, inhaling the scouring cold, the sea salt, amazed still that the ocean was so close, the smell of it everywhere. She headed for it, passing candy-colored Victorian homes festooned with gingerbread trim, trying to imagine what the streets would be like at the height of the summer season, packed with oily bodies in shorts and bathing suits, little kids sticky with sand and cotton candy.

Lily crossed Beach Drive, climbed the steps to the promenade—a wide sidewalk snaking alongside the shore—and sat on one of the benches looking out over the sea. It was way too cold for beachgoers, too cold for the gulls even. The sand looked clean and white and soft, and Lily couldn't resist it.

She picked a dry spot near the gray sand marked by the tide and sat, watching as the surf came up and licked at her toes. She pulled off her knit gloves and scooped up some of the sand in her palm, using a shell to dig up more sand and form it until she had the shape of something, a house. Packing the icy sand tightly with her numb fingers, she flattened rooftops, carved windows and a door with a small twig, erasing her mistakes with droplets of water. The wind whipped her long hair out from her head like a sail, and she shook it away so that she could see.

A lone man in a long dark coat and brimmed hat stood still as a statue on the promenade. She squinted but could not make out his face beneath the hat. Her skin, already raw from the cold, rippled on her arms as the man continued to stare. What could he be looking at? *Who* could he be looking at? She glanced around, but there was nobody else on the beach. The sea was gray and boatless, the sky a dull shade of blue. *Maybe he just likes beaches*, she told herself. *Maybe he likes the ocean.*

Maybe he was the man who had been in her house.

Lily shook her head—*forget the man, forget the Kewpie, forget Montclair*—adding windows and a front walk to the house. It was a while before she dared to look up again. Where the man once stood, there was a blond-haired girl wrestling with a dark-haired boy, both of them giggling madly. The sound made her limbs go quivery with loneliness. Even though she was far from the promenade, she could tell one of the wrestlers was Broken-Nose Boy, and she turned away quickly, grabbing handfuls of her own hair and shoving it down the back of her coat so that he wouldn't see it. See her building a sand castle like some dopey little kid. But she didn't care how stupid it was. It was a good house, the best. She looked then at what she had built and saw that one of the levels, the smaller one, had caved in. She must have knocked it with her elbow or her foot when she turned away from the boy and the blonde; now she'd ruined everything.

why can't you WHY CAN'T YOU why can't you WHY CAN'T YOU why can'

"Why can't you ever watch what you're doing? You just wrecked that little girl's sand castle!" said the woman, the floppy flowers on her bathing cap ruffled by some strange wind.

"What do you want me to do? I tripped, okay? That creep with the feathered hat was digging a darned hole again. Somebody oughta do something about him."

But the woman simply glared at her husband. "Why don't you apologize to the girl instead of standing there like a fool?"

"All right, all right," the man said. "Keep your shirt on." He turned to the girl. "Sorry about your castle—there, little girl. My eyes aren't too good anymore."

"Oh, dear, now she's upset!" the woman said. "Do something!"

"What do you want me to do?" the man bellowed. "Mix some cement?"

"Buy her a soda or a pretzel or something."

"The concession stand isn't open yet."

"Oh, dear."

"She'll get over it," said the man. "Kids always do."

Pink

*L*ola lolled like the Cheshire Cat on top of the kitchen table, plotting glorious plots, scheming delicious schemes.

Now that she'd moved into the old Victorian, looked around, got comfy, she saw that things were so much more unfair than she first thought. Totally, absolutely unfair.

Steffie was rich. Maybe her dad was a science geek, too, and had invented some scientific thingamajiggy that made a trillion dollars. The house was huge and filled with all kinds of ugly but mondo expensive stuff. Steffie the role stealer got to star in *Damn Yankees* and then come home to eat caviar off three-hundred-year-old china plates and drink champagne out of flutes hand-blown for French kings. Not that Lola had seen Steffie or her mother ever eating caviar—they ate lots of *pancakes,* the cheeseballs—but she was totally sure they could afford to if they wanted.

That was not right.

And then there was the guy. The totally gorgeous guy. Lola hadn't got a good look at him until he was right in front of her, but even with the smushed schnozz and the blood, she practically fell into those soulful eyes. Lola figured a studmuffin like that wouldn't ever dig a loser like Steffie. He'd dig someone . . . well, someone like Lola. And he would have been totally into Lola, she was sure of it, if he had just been able to *see* her. She had sung at the top of her lungs; she had posed at the top of the stairs; she'd performed a kicky, Fosse-inspired dance number on the porch; but of course he hadn't noticed any of it. Being dead was the pits. She was so mad that she'd had to trip Steffie just to make the day worth living.

Ha! Living!

Lola rolled over onto her back, gnashing her teeth at the little Siamese that seemed to be frowning at her from the windowsill. Cats were so judgmental. "Shoo!" she said. "Why don't you go bother one of the others? It's not like I'm the only ghost around here." The Human Candle, for example. Something totally wrong with that guy. Creeped her out.

The cat gave a stern little mewl of disapproval, jumped down from the sill, and sauntered off, tail in the air. Lola bet it wouldn't act so snotty if she spray painted it pink.

Pink, she thought. That was the ticket. A little makeover, a little drama, a little color in a dead gray world. She had done it before. Like on that other girl who Lola was positive was Steffie but turned out to be some bank teller or whatever. (So many people looked and acted *exactly* like Steffie. Dozens, literally. Lola was amazed. The weirdest one was that forty-four-year-old mother of two. Lola was still a tad embarrassed about that mistake; she hoped the woman's eyebrows were growing in okay.)

She jumped down from the table and did a foxy little shimmy and a couple of high kicks before hopping down the steps into the basement. "Just what I was looking for," she said. "Mr. Washer, Mr. Dryer." She opened up the washer. "Whites! How very convenient. Oops!" she said, scooping a bright red sweater from the laundry basket and dropping it into the washer. After adding half a bottle of dish soap, she pulled the nozzle to start the wash, doing a hula to the slushy, sloshy sound of the water.

Lola wiggled and Lola sang, imagining the red dye seeping out of the sweater and onto the rest of the white, white clothes.

A little pink goes a long way, she thought. She wondered how far a *lot* of pink would go.

Chapter 5

As she had promised, Lily's mother tossed the Kewpie into the closet with Uncle Max. "So Julep can't play any more of her little tricks." Lily spent the next couple of weeks doing algebra and struggling with literature, all the while keeping an eye on the windows and the doors. Except for the crank phone calls, no one in the town seemed to be interested in spying on them or even finding out who they were. Still, Lily was bored and uneasy. When she got too bored and too uneasy, she went down to the beach and carved little worlds out of the frigid sand.

Lily sat at the dining-room table, trying to make sense of the book she had to read, *The Old Man and the Sea*, while Julep rolled a pen around on the floor. There weren't many books Lily liked. They all seemed so unreal, the people saying such perfect things. Who says perfect things all the time? Her mother had tried to explain it to her. "Books aren't life, they're better. They distill life. Books are life with all the boring parts cut out." Her mother had made up essay questions, which Lily thought was a terrible thing to do to your own kid.

In her opinion, Hemingway had cut none of the boring parts out of *The Old Man and the Sea*. The entire thing was a giant snore. Some guy goes fishing. He catches a big fish. He tows it to shore, but sharks eat it before he gets there. What was that supposed to mean?

She gave up on the book, turned on the TV, and whipped through the channels. The dialogue blurred into one long, babbling sentence: "Oh, Aurelia, tell me you love—," "A doll like this could fetch thousands from—" "People who have been searching New Jersey beaches for everything from quarters to pirate treasure to—" "Tell me you love me, tell me you love me, tell me you love me!"

The doorbell rang. It was a high, sweet chirping, like a bird. It didn't go with the house. Lily had expected a trumpeting sound. Or maybe a gong.

She scowled when she looked through the peephole and saw who it was, but she unlocked the door anyway, and flung it open. "What do you want?"

Broken-Nose Boy blinked. "Hello to you, too." He held out her sweatshirt. "I wanted to bring you this. I think I got all the blood out."

Lily looked down at the sweatshirt, surprised. "Thanks," she said. "I didn't expect you to bring it back."

"I know," he said, smiling.

Lily took the shirt. She wasn't sure what to make of this and was worried that he had come to tease her about sand castles and ratty old clothes.

"My mom told me to soak it in water and hand soap with a little ammonia," he said. He gestured at the shirt she was wearing. "Maybe it would work for that one, too."

Lily looked down at her once-white shirt, now covered in huge pink blotches. "It's not blood. A red sweater got mixed in with the whites. Everything I own is like this. It's my new look, okay?"

"Oh," he said. "Sorry."

"Well, thanks," she said, and started to close the door.

"Wait," he said. "Look, I think we started off all wrong. I'm Vaz." And he held out his hand. Lily had never shaken hands with anyone her own age. His was an ice cube.

"What's your name?" he asked.

"Lily."

Vaz nodded. "That makes sense."

"What do you mean?"

"You look like one, kind of. It might be the hair. Like a tiger lily. My mom plants those everywhere."

She had no idea what to say, especially with him standing there smiling shyly, so focused in on his slanted nose instead. Even though she was still annoyed with him, she hoped that she wasn't the one who had slanted it.

"How's the nose?"

"Sore, but it works okay." He put his hands in his pockets and shivered. A breeze lifted a curl off his forehead, where it stood like a question mark.

"Do you want to come in?" Lily said reluctantly. "It's kind of cold out here."

"Thanks," Vaz said, and stepped inside.

She shut the door behind him. "I was just going to make some hot chocolate," she said, though she had just thought of it. "You want some?"

"Sure." He followed her down the hallway, through the dining room, and into the kitchen. She pulled out some instant hot chocolate, saw him gaping at the dining room and parlor before she turned to fill some mugs with water. "I've never been inside one of these houses before," he said from the doorway. "I didn't think it would be so fancy."

"It's not my house, remember? It's my great-uncle's."

"Still, what's it like to live in this kind of place?"

"You can't sit on any of the furniture, and the maids are always mouthing off."

"You have maids?" he said.

"I was making a joke." She had no idea why, since she wasn't very funny.

Lily heated the mugs of water in the microwave and stirred the mix into the water, then brought the mugs into the dining room.

He took off his coat and put it gingerly over the back of one of the dining-room chairs. "Is this okay?"

"Well, I don't think your coat is going to break it."

"Guess not," he said, and laughed, which pleased her despite herself. He looked down at the table. "Are these your books?"

"Yeah."

"No one stole them today, huh?" He must have caught her scowl because he held up both hands. "Hey, I'm just kidding." He thumbed through *The Old Man and the Sea.* "I remember this book. It's a good book."

He had surprised her again—first, because he read books; second, because he had such bad taste in them. "I think it's a terrible book," she said.

"Why?"

"Some old fisherman catches a fish and the sharks eat it. Who cares?"

"Oh, no," said Vaz. "No. The guy's not just a fisherman. He's a hero. He battles against nature and wins."

"A bunch of sharks *eat* his fish. How is that winning?"

"He caught the fish, didn't he?"

"Yeah, so?"

He smiled at her with his big white teeth. "You've never been fishing, have you?"

"How did you guess?"

He took a sip of the hot chocolate. "My dad was a fisherman." He tapped his own chest. "I'm from a long line of Greek guys who make their living on the water. He used to say that we go all the way back to Odysseus."

"Who?"

"Odysseus. From *The Odyssey*? It's this book about a guy who sails around for twenty years battling monsters and sorceresses, trying to get home."

"I must have missed that one." Lily didn't add that when she did read something, she never remembered much about it later. All that made-up stuff. Who cared about made-up people?

Vaz put the book back onto the table. "*The Old Man and the Sea* is pretty cool."

"The sharks were cool, anyway," Lily said.

They sipped their hot chocolates, not saying anything for a few minutes. Lily sneaked looks at the boy. Even with the crooked nose, he was nice to look at. She wondered how she looked to him, if she really looked like a flower. She touched her hair, hoping that the bun on top of her head didn't resemble a nest thrown together by spastic birds.

Lily racked her brain for something to say. "So, you're Greek? Like born in Greece Greek?"

"No, like born in South Jersey Greek. Actually, I'm only half, the big nose, dark skin half. My mom's Irish with a bunch of other stuff thrown in." He put his hands around the mug. "How come you don't go to school?"

"My mom's homeschooling me."

"No way."

Lily shrugged. "Better than going to junior high."

"Junior high's not so bad."

"Yeah? What about your smashed nose?"

"Oh, well." Vaz frowned. "That's different."

"What happened?"

"Nah. It's nothing. Stupid stuff. Hey, she's cute. Come here, kitty."

Lily watched as Julep abandoned her pen and wandered over to Vaz for a scratch under the chin. A fight over some girl, Lily thought, some cheerleader who looked like a Barbie, not a lily. Like the blond girl on the boardwalk.

The phone rang. Lily ignored it. It rang again, and then a third time.

"Aren't you going to get the phone?"

She shook her head. "We get a lot of crank calls."

"Kids? 'Is your refrigerator running? You better go catch it!'"

"Not that kind of crank call. The kind where you pick up the phone and no one's there."

"That's weird. Want me to answer it? I can make my voice really deep. Sometimes it scares them off."

"Sure, if you want."

"Where's the phone?"

Lily pointed. Vaz walked over to the ornate phone in the parlor and picked up the receiver. "Hello," he croaked, grinning at Lily. He listened for a moment, the smile dropping off his face. He hung up the phone, then stood staring at it as if he thought it might get up and run away.

He cleared his throat. "I thought you said that the cranks never say anything."

"They never did before."

"Well, he just said something."

Lily put her mug on the table. "What did he say?"

Vaz looked at her, brows furrowed. "'Hit the road, Odysseus.'"

Chapter 6

L ily's mouth was so dry, it felt like she'd swallowed a cupful of sand. "Are you sure that's what they said? 'Hit the road, Odysseus'?"

"Yes, I'm sure."

"I knew somebody was spying on us. I knew it! It must be the same person I saw peeking at us through the window that day I met you. And the same person who moved my books."

"Maybe. But why would someone want to spy on you?"

"I don't know."

Vaz pulled his coat from the back of the chair. "Come on," he said.

"Where are we going?"

"We're going to take a look around outside. Maybe we can catch whoever it is."

The gravel driveway crunched under their shoes as she and Vaz made their way around the side of the house to the backyard. The yard was large but not huge, and there were only a few trees and hedges that a would-be spy could hide behind.

Lily shivered and clutched her collar tighter. "Maybe he's not spying from outside. Maybe he's spying from another house. Maybe he has binoculars or a telescope or something."

"How could he hear what we were saying, then?" Vaz said. "How would he know we were talking about Odysseus?"

"Maybe he reads lips."

"Maybe he reads minds," Vaz said.

"Well, you tell me how it happened."

Vaz ran his hands through his hair. "Are you sure you can't think of any reason why someone would spy on you?"

"There's nothing."

"What about your mom? What does she do?"

"She's not a government agent."

"I'm serious," he said.

"She makes jewelry, okay? And it's *weird* jewelry. There aren't a lot of people all that interested in what she does."

"What about your dad?"

Lily stared. "What about him?"

"Where is he?"

"He doesn't live here," Lily said. She wasn't about to explain. People understood dead. People understood divorce. They didn't understand gone.

"Okay," Vaz said. "What about you?"

"What about me?"

"Why would somebody want to spy on you?"

"Maybe they weren't spying on me," Lily said. "Maybe they were spying on *you*. Maybe you're some kind of teenage drug dealer. Maybe you fence stolen silverware and TV sets. Maybe you're an alien and the government wants to dissect you."

"Okay, okay," Vaz said. "Never mind. I'm sorry I asked."

Neither of them moved until Lily decided that if she had to be scared and paranoid, then it was better if she were scared and paranoid and warm. They went back inside and sat at the kitchen table.

Vaz kept his coat on, as if a coat could protect him from whoever was watching them. He drummed his fingers on the table. "So, your uncle's letting you stay here, huh? What's he like?"

"Don't know. I never met him." Lily tugged on a rope of her hair. "At least, I don't remember ever meeting him."

"You never met your own uncle?"

"It's my mom's uncle. And anyway, she hasn't seen him in years. She hasn't seen any of her family in years."

"Why not?"

Lily had asked her mother that question hundreds of times. "Because they don't approve of my choices," her mother told her. "Because they think that money is the most important thing in the world. But money's not everything." And then she would talk about love and hope and art and dreams. "People need to dream," said Lily's mother, "or else they die."

But then, the year Lily was ten, her mother's parents did die, one after the other, and Lily stopped asking questions.

To Vaz, Lily said, "We're here now. I guess whatever reasons my mom had aren't as big a deal as she thought they were."

Vaz unzipped his coat. "So, besides chasing creeps who break into your house, what do you like to do?"

Lily almost said, "Look at weird things under a microscope" but caught herself; she didn't have a microscope anymore. "I don't know. Regular stuff. Baby-sit. Sometimes I help my mom when she sells her jewelry at a show or whatever."

"That's work. What do you like to do when you don't have to work?"

Lily blinked. She mostly did things she had to do, not liked to do. "I don't know."

"Let me guess." He leaned back and studied her. "You paint."

She hadn't painted anything in years, unless she was forced to in art class. "No."

"Hmmm," he said. "You're a dancer. One of those dancers who makes like a tree or an egg. A modern dancer." He stood and assumed a tree pose, arms extended like branches.

She smiled. He was too goofy. "Uh . . . no."

"Okay. You write things. Poetry. About your tortured adolescence, your twisted mind."

She giggled. "No," she said, but she wished she had a twisted mind. It sounded kind of fun.

"No, you don't write poetry, or no, you don't write about your tortured adolescence?"

"You know what I mean."

He took off his coat and sat. "You're a cheerleader."

"No."

"A bandleader."

"No."

"A ringleader."

"A what?"

He grinned even wider. "I know what you are. You're

one of those girls who has a zillion boyfriends in eighteen different states, aren't you?"

"No," she said, laughing and blushing furiously.

"Sure you are," he said. "No wonder you don't have time to paint."

She burst out laughing.

"Now it's your turn," he said. "Guess what I like to do."

"I have no clue," she said. He looked like the kind of person who could do anything.

"Come on, guess."

"I don't know, bake cakes?"

"Close. I *eat* cakes. Guess again."

She leaned back in her chair and looked him over the way he'd looked her over, hoping that she looked as cool and relaxed as he had. His hands looked about four sizes too big for his tall, skinny body. "You play basketball," she said.

"Close," he said. "I *eat* basketballs."

She winced and laughed at the same time. "You're really strange."

"Right!" he said. "Exactly right! How did you guess?"

She caught a glimpse of herself in the mirrored cabinet over Vaz's head: the open-mouthed grin, the flushed face and mussed hair. Ugh. She looked like she just rolled out of bed after a long, muggy night, which embarrassed her so much she leaped to her feet.

He gazed up at her. "I guess I should be going anyway."

"Oh, sorry, I was just—"

"No problem." He checked his watch. "My mom will wonder what happened to me." He put on his coat. "As long as you're all right."

"What do you mean?"

"The crank call, remember?"

"Oh!" she said. She'd completely forgotten about it. "It was only a phone call."

"Still, it's pretty weird."

"Yeah," she said, trying to sound flip, unconcerned. "But my mom will be home soon. We'll figure something out." She walked him to the front door.

"Well," he said. "It's been . . . interesting."

"Yeah," she said. "Interesting."

"I'll see you around?"

She looked at her feet. "Maybe."

He grinned and walked out, taking the stairs in one leap.

She shut the door behind him. All of a sudden the house was deadly quiet and she felt soft and out of breath, like a balloon with a slow leak.

As she hung up her coat, she thought about the phone call. Maybe Vaz hadn't heard right. Maybe it was just a wrong number. Not "Hit the road, Odysseus," but "Is this Missus . . . ?" or whatever.

But just in case there was a real spy, Lily went around the house pulling down all the shades and closing all of the curtains. With each window she got more annoyed with herself, more annoyed with Vaz. Now that he'd hung out with her once, talked to her, been nice to her, all she would think about was when he would come back.

Uh-oh. You like him. You know what that means, don't you? Moodiness. Loss of appetite. Sniveling. Makeup.

"I know," said Lily, frowning hard enough to hurt. "I know."

Chapter 7

A few days after Vaz came by, her mother had a surprise. "Guess who called today? Guess who's coming to dinner? To see us? Tonight? In a half hour?"

"Uh, Odysseus?"

"Uncle Wes!" Her mother looked as if she had swallowed a large, leggy bug. "Isn't that nice?"

"If you say so," said Lily, because her mother had always acted as if family members were something to be respected but avoided, like bears or gainful employment. "What are you cooking?"

"Who's cooking?" said her mother, holding up two plastic bags. Thai takeout.

Lily looked at the bags. "Does Uncle Wes like Thai food?"

The bags sank to the floor. "Doesn't everybody?"

From her mother's description of Wes, Lily had expected some shuffling twig of a thing. But Uncle Wes was tall and spry, with silver hair combed back from a high, unlined forehead. One eye was green, the other a peculiar icy blue; both stared down a strong, bony nose.

The three of them settled themselves as best they could in the stiff parlor furniture. Lily's backside promptly fell asleep.

Uncle Wes cleared his throat. "You're looking well,

Arden. Young as ever."

"Thank you, Wes," Lily's mother said. "You look well . . . as well."

Uncle Wes appraised Lily from his perch in one of the Chippendales. Lily felt she should say something about somebody looking well, but she didn't know which of Wes's eyes to focus on, so found herself bouncing from the blue one to the green one like an anxious bee.

"She looks like her father," Wes said finally.

Lily's mother crossed one leg over the other. "Yes, she does."

"But she's tall," he said. "Now, that's from our line." This time he addressed Lily instead of her mother. "Your grandmother was tall. And my brother."

"Max?" said Lily.

"Maxmillian," he corrected. He rubbed his hands together briskly. "Do you feel a draft in here?"

"I'll turn up the heat if you like," said Lily's mother.

"Don't bother," he said. "I'm fine." He clasped his hands on his lap. He wore jeans but wore them awkwardly, like a man used to a suit.

"How do you like Cape May?"

"It's very nice," Lily's mother said. "Very, *very* nice," she added.

"And Lily, how's school so far?"

Lily wriggled in her seat, hoping to wake up her butt. "Um . . . I don't go to school."

"Excuse me?" Uncle Wes frowned at Lily's mother.

"I wanted to let Lily get settled in," her mother said. "I've been tutoring her at home."

"My mom's a great teacher," said Lily.

"Well," he said, clearly appalled. "I'm sure she is."

"How about dinner?" Lily's mother said brightly. "I thought we'd sit in the dining room."

Uncle Wes stood. "Oh, I wouldn't want you to make a fuss. The kitchen is fine."

"It's no trouble. I already set the table. See?" Lily's mother pointed through the archway. "You two sit, and I'll get the food."

Lily plunked herself into a dining-room chair, but Wes stood behind his. He seemed to be dazed by the glittering chandelier, almost mesmerized.

"What's the matter?" Lily asked.

A small muscle beneath his blue eye twitched. "The chandelier is beautiful, isn't it? It was my mother's favorite piece in the whole house. I can't help but think of her when I look at it."

"Was she nice?" Lily asked. "Your mother?"

"Of course," he said. "But not to everyone."

It was just the kind of thing her own mother might have said, and Lily struggled not to cluck her tongue in disgust.

Uncle Wes took a seat just as Lily's mother swept into the room laden with platters. Uncle Wes looked at plates piled with red and green curries, spicy rice noodles, and thin-skinned dumplings with such a dismayed expression that Lily felt a bit sorry for him.

"Oh, my," he said. "The food is quite . . . exotic."

Her mother's mouth caved in, so that for a moment she looked like a woman without teeth. "I'm sure I can find something else."

"Oh, I wouldn't hear of it," said Wes, pulling a linen napkin out of a gold ring and placing it across his lap. "I'm sure it's delicious. Whatever it is." He dug into the curries gamely.

Lily's mother whispered, "Go get your uncle some water. A lot of water."

Your uncle, your uncle, Lily thought as she filled a glass of water at the kitchen sink. Lily wasn't sure if she liked him, and it made her feel weird. Weren't you supposed to like your family? She imagined meeting her father again. What if she didn't like him? What if he didn't like her?

She heard a splashing sound and gasped. The sink was filled to the brim, the water spilling all over the floor.

"Whoa!" she said, jumping back.

"Lily? Are you all right?"

"Yes!" she called. Frantic, she put the glass down before grabbing both faucets and turning them first clockwise, then counterclockwise. The water shot from the spigot as if she'd done nothing at all.

"Lily? The water?"

A rivulet snaked toward the door. Towels. She needed towels, she thought, yanking yards of paper towels from the roll on the wall.

"Earth to Lily," her mother sang.

She looked down. The floor was dry, the sink empty. The water glass sat on the counter, full.

"What?" she said out loud. "What?" Seeing things again! What was with her? Mental illness? Early Alzheimer's?

"Lily!"

She crumpled the paper towels into a ball and threw them in the garbage can. "Coming!"

She set the water in front of Uncle Wes, and he nearly drained the glass. "Thank you," he said.

He choked down some more curry. "You may not look like your mother, but I'm sure you're just as smart as she is. What kinds of things do you like to do?"

Vaz had just asked her that question, and she figured she better work on some better answers. *I enjoy skydiving, spelunking, and seeing things that aren't there.*

"I like the ocean," she said.

Uncle Wes leaned forward, intrigued. "Really? My brother loved the ocean. He had all kinds of books. Seafarers and adventurers and pirates, that sort of thing."

"I'm more interested in animals. Sharks. And giant squid. Did you know that the biggest giant squid ever found was fifty-five feet long? No one's ever seen a live one. Not an adult squid, anyway. I'd like to."

"Fascinating," said Uncle Wes. He glanced at his plate as if he were worried that some giant squid was mixed in with the noodles. "But you'll need money to find your big squid, won't you? How will you support yourself?"

"Oh, I'm going to be rich," said Lily.

Uncle Wes coughed and had to sip more water. "Rich? Really? How will you manage that?"

Lily wasn't sure how she'd manage it—all she knew was that she had to. She wasn't going to live hand-to-mouth the rest of her life, all dreams and nothing to finance them.

She shrugged. "I don't know how. I just will."

Uncle Wes stared at her curiously, then set his napkin next to his plate. He shivered.

"Is something wrong?" Lily's mother asked.

"No, no. I think I should replace these old windows soon." He rubbed his own arms.

"If you're finished eating, I can light a fire."

"A fire would be wonderful. Thank you. I'll admit I'm chilled to the bone."

Uncle Wes insisted on fetching the firewood from the porch and starting the fire himself. "Man's greatest invention, fire," he said. Lily and her mother gave him the armchair closest to the fireplace.

Lily, feeling rather warm and cozy, pulled off her sweater and stretched out on the couch as her mother and Uncle Wes chatted about operas and symphonies and wines. The rich, earthy smell of smoke made her feel dazed and sleepy.

"Would you like a blanket?" she heard her mother say.

"I don't know why I'm so cold," said Uncle Wes. "I'm right next to the fire. And you two seem comfortable."

Lily opened her eyes just a bit and thought she saw a hazy fog of condensation emanating from her uncle's mouth, as if he were outside rather than in. The fire was miniaturized in his eyes.

Julep chose that moment for one of her ecstatic kitty fits and thundered into the room, batting something—a washer? a quarter?—under the couch. She jumped up on the armchair and gaped, showing Uncle Wes her pointy teeth. He jumped from the chair.

"What a charming creature," he said, appalled yet again.

"Lily, why don't you take Julep upstairs with you?" her mother said.

"Yes," said Uncle Wes. "I'm sure it's getting close to your bedtime."

Lily could clearly see his breath now, she was sure of it, and it made her shudder though she wasn't cold. She gave her mother a kiss good-night and then turned to Uncle Wes.

"It was nice meeting you, Uncle Wes," she said. She stepped closer to him, right into a wall of frigid air, air that smelled of ash, of soot.

"It's cold!" she said.

"That's what I've been saying," he said, irritably now. "It's very cold."

Yes, Lily thought, *but why only around you?*

-bitty baby and strawberry jam ITTY-BITTY BABY AND STRAWBERRY JAM

Itty~Bitty Baby and Strawberry Jam

*L*ola watched Steffie sleep curled up in an itty-bitty ball, her itchy-witchy hair hanging off the edge of the bed.

Dweeb-o-rama goes to dreamland.

Lola strolled around the room. Where was the geek stuff? Geeks always had crazy little machines to smash. Model airplanes or gizmos that converted sugar to gasoline or whatever. Tiny working volcanoes. But Steffie didn't have any of that kind of stuff. Steffie didn't have any of *anything*.

Lola had been planning to arrange all of Steffie's shoes into a room-sized smiley face—a weird little surprise for when she woke up—but the gackmonster had only three pairs. What kind of loser had just three pairs of shoes? She opened the closet to pull all the clothes off the hangers, but the hangers were empty. All the clothes seemed to be in a couple of skanky duffel bags on the floor. And then there were only a few sweatshirts, a few pairs of jeans.

If Lola were her, she'd just grab a handful of silverware and take it to the junk shop for some cash. Buy something decent to wear. Leg warmers. Pumps. A bitchin' miniskirt or two.

Lola herself had grabbed a silver spoon from the dining room, and now she plunged it into a jumbo jar of strawberry jam. Steffie didn't make a sound as Lola filled all three pairs of her shoes with Nature's Best fruit preserves. Then she reached into one of the duffels and pulled out a flannel shirt. She wrapped the jelly jar with the shirt and buried it at the bottom of the bag. Mold city.

She was bored again.

She'd been bored all night, mostly because Sir Flame-a-Lot wouldn't let her get near Steffie. No, he had to hog the haunt-ings, pasting himself to that tall old guy, Steffie's grandpop or whatever, getting in the old guy's face, freezing him with frigid ghostie ectoplasm. Lame. (Though she had to admit the trick with the water was pretty gnarly.)

Really, if he weren't such a meanie, Lola probably would have helped him fulfill his every malicious wish. But every time she came near he'd start waving his torch hands around and doing his crazy dance, and Lola wasn't going to be a part of that loco little show, no way! She was stuck chasing the cat for entertain-ment. Of course Mr. No Fun for Anyone Else had put the kibosh on that, too, when he gave the cat the coin to play with.

Oh, well. A party is what you make it, right? Lola dove back into the duffel bag. She unearthed the jam jar, still a quarter full, and turned back to Steffie, who slumbered away.

Lola grinned. *Sweets to the sweet!*

Chapter 8

Lily woke up to the sound of voices and bolted upright, imagining dolls and cascading water and gaping mouths like broken windows. The moon was high in her window, casting an eerie light around the room. The air was thick with the smell of strawberries.

And there was something wrong with her face.

She stumbled out of bed and ran for the door, wiping her hands across her cheeks. A gritty, sticky paste came away in her palms. She opened the door and heard her mother and Uncle Wes.

"Arden, you must! I insist. She's only a child."

"Yes, she's only a child. *My* child."

"At least let me give you something. Buy her some decent clothes. Some books. Whatever she needs."

Her mother's voice was ragged. "We just need a place to stay for a while, that's all. I don't need your money. *We* don't need your money."

"Well, if you're certain," he said. "All you have to do is ask, you know."

"Thank you," said Lily's mother, sounding not very thankful at all.

"Good night, Arden."

"Good night, Wesley."

Lily was creeping across the hallway to the bathroom when she heard her mother crying.

Her face had been slathered with some kind of fruit preserve that took fifteen minutes to get off. And she'd stumbled back into her room to find her shoes filled with more of the same. Who would have done such a thing? Who could have? It didn't make any sense. She crouched in bed all night until the shadows dancing along the walls seemed to gather and roil into a single humpbacked shape that waddled like an oversized possum in the corners of her room.

The next morning she ran downstairs to tell her mother about the jam, but she saw her mother's red-rimmed eyes and quivering mouth and felt the words dying on her tongue. How could she tell her mother, upsetting her more, when she hardly believed it herself?

Left alone in the creepy house after her mother went to the shop, Lily distracted herself with activity. She played with the cat. She did two math chapters. She swept the floors and scrubbed the sink. She watched a TV special on poison jellyfish and another on Captain Kidd. She avoided the basement.

As she warmed up some leftover Thai for lunch, Lily thought that what bothered her most wasn't that weird stuff was happening, but that it was happening to *her*. Lily hadn't had a nightmare since she was five years old; she yawned at scary books and movies. Her mother sometimes accused her of having no imagination at all, and Lily had been pleased by the comment. It meant that she wouldn't—couldn't—be fooled.

Julep jumped up on the kitchen table, trying to get a whiff of the noodles, but Lily shooed her away. The cat managed to produce a look so aggrieved and human that Lily said, "Oh, get over it. You don't even like spicy food. And it will just give you bad kitty breath."

The doorbell chirped. Lily felt a tiny burst of hope in her chest, and she quashed it down. *It could just be the mailman, you know.* She pressed her eye to the peephole.

It wasn't the mailman. It was Vaz.

She threw open the door. "Hi," she said.

"Hi," Vaz said. He was carrying a backpack and a basketball. "I just wanted to see if you were around."

"Yeah, I'm around." She stepped aside so that he could come in.

He wrinkled his nose. "What's that smell?"

She covered her mouth with her hand as they walked to the kitchen. "We had pad Thai for dinner last night," she said. "I was just eating the leftovers."

He took off his jacket and looked curiously at the food. "It looks a little like Chinese. Is it good?"

"Yeah," said Lily. "I like it, anyway. You've never had Thai?"

"I didn't even know that we had a Thai restaurant," Vaz said, spinning the basketball on the tip of his finger. "I thought this town was strictly fish and steak and baked potatoes. My dad used to make great souvlaki—it's lamb. Like a shish kebob. I bet you never had souvlaki."

"Sure I have."

He stopped spinning the basketball. "You have?"

"Yeah," she said, happy that she knew what souvlaki was, that she had tried it. "There was a Greek place around the corner from me when I lived in Chicago. We went there all the time."

"Chicago. Right," he said, the look on his face half surprise, half admiration. "I've never been to Chicago." He peered at the food again.

"Do you want to try it?"

"Uh . . . I don't know." He put the basketball on the chair.

"Yes, you do." Lily got a saucer and a fork, put a little bit of the pad Thai on the plate, and watched him take a bite.

"It's good," he said. "What's in here? Peanuts?" He scooped up another bite and swallowed. In two minutes, the saucer was clean.

"Do you want the rest?" Lily asked.

"No," he said. "That's okay. I know you were eating."

"I was just going to throw it out."

"In that case . . ." He grabbed the little white container and grinned. "I wouldn't want it to go to waste."

He finished the leftovers in four or five large bites. "Thanks. That was really good." He put the container down on the table, gestured at Julep, who was eyeing him from a chair.

"Your cat's giving me a dirty look."

"Oh, well. That's because I wouldn't let her have some." Lily finished her fruit punch and pointed to the basketball. "I was right. You *do* play basketball."

"Yup," Vaz said. "But not that well."

Lily didn't like doing things she didn't do well. "So why do you play?"

"Nothing better to do, I guess. I'd like to play tennis, but it's too cold. Do you play tennis?"

"Badly. Very badly."

"That's okay," he said. "When it gets warmer, I'll teach you." He grabbed at the collar of his shirt and tugged at it. "Speaking of warmer, does it feel kinda hot in here?"

"I guess," Lily said. But then, it did feel warmer. Steamy, too, like the air before a storm. Why would it be so humid all of a sudden? "The food," she said, annoyed when she heard the relief in her own voice. "The spicy food always does that." Last night, Uncle Wes had been freezing.

"The food was spicy," Vaz said. He pressed his napkin to his upper lip, where sweat had begun to bead.

"How about water," Lily said, her brain chattering, *Water, yeah, that's what we need, water will fix it.* Her head felt woozy, as if she had a fever.

She got up and threw her punch cup in the sink, opened a cabinet, and fumbled with water glasses that weighed as much as small dumbbells, almost pitching them to the floor. Vaz was making her nervous, that's all. She filled the glasses, sloshing water over her forearm, wondering if she should just stick her whole head under the spigot, wake herself up.

She brought the glasses to the table, and Vaz downed

his in one long pull. She sipped at hers. The air felt dense somehow, thick, and her own movements were slow and clumsy. What was wrong with her? The sun shone through the windows, the cat washed her face with her paw, everything in the room looked the same—so why was her skin prickling? What did her skin know that her brain didn't? Her nose filled with a sweet, waxy scent.

"Do you smell lipstick?" she blurted out.

"I didn't know lipstick had a smell."

"It does," she said lamely. "Sort of." Seeing, hearing, and now *smelling* things. She got up and put their glasses in the dishwasher, then came back to the table. Julep stopped washing in midstream, paw up, ears twitching. Her shiny pupils had widened to swallow most of her irises, and for a moment Lily thought she saw tiny blue flames reflected in the deep black pools.

Lily's lips felt slick and greasy, and she wiped at them with her hand. "The food—" she began, but Vaz's shocked expression killed the words in the back of her throat. "What?"

He opened and closed his mouth a few times, then said, "What—what did you do to your face?"

"Huh? What are you talking about?" She glanced behind him to the mirrored cabinets. Some kind of bright pink color was smeared around her mouth, making it look raw and burned.

Lily grabbed her napkin and tried to wipe the mess off her face as her mind jabbered, *How did the lipstick get on my face? How? How? How?* For a second the air got even warmer, thicker, before a stiff chill wind swept through the room, bringing with it a sooty, acrid scent, like a barbecue doused by rain.

"Did you feel that?" Vaz said. "Is a window open or something?"

"No," Lily said. "No windows."

A cold puff of air filled Lily's ear, and she flinched against it as if it were a knife. She could feel her skin tensing into gooseflesh, her stomach twisting into a chemical knot. Somewhere, somebody moaned.

"Is that you?" Vaz asked, alarm pinching his face. "Who is that?"

"I don't know," Lily said. There was another chill and ragged breath, and another, and another. Lily twisted away, frantically rubbing her earlobe.

Vaz dropped the basketball. "Is that breathing? Are you breathing like that?"

"No," Lily whispered. The sound was slow and hushed at first, like the low sighing of someone sleeping in the next room, but then it gathered momentum: inhale, exhale, inhale, exhale. The fur on Julep's back bristled, and her tail grew twice the size. She hissed before she tore out of the room, claws scratching on the wood floor.

Lily threw her napkin on the table, suddenly furious. She would not be scared. She would *not*. "Who's breathing like that?" Lily demanded. She twisted in her chair, then got up and charged around the kitchen. "Who are you? Where are you?"

But the breathing got louder and louder and louder, huffing into panting, panting into roaring, until she had to clap her hands over her ears to drown it out. Vaz grabbed one of her wrists and dragged her out the back door to the deck, slamming the door shut with his foot.

"Oh, man," he said, shaking his head. "You got ghosts."

Chapter 9

Lily glared at the wrist where Vaz held her, and he let go as if she were in danger of exploding.

"Ghosts?" she said as soon as she could catch her breath. "You can't be serious."

"How else can you explain it?"

"What do you mean, how else can I explain it?" she said. "I can explain it in a thousand ways! There was somebody else in the house! There was somebody in the window! There was somebody in the kitchen or the hallway!" *Yeah, but how did the jam get into your shoes? How did that pink get all over your face?* She imagined the Kewpie doing a little soft-shoe shuffle in the closet.

He stared at her mouth. "We were the only people in the kitchen."

"I can't believe I'm hearing this." Lily wanted to cry in fear and confusion.

"My grandmother lived in a house with the ghost of a parrot," he said. "Late at night, you could hear the parrot calling for its owner. Turtle Bunny."

"Turtle Bunny."

"That's what the parrot called the guy who owned her. Turtle Bunny."

Lily sat on the edge of the deck. "Are you sure you

didn't take a decongestant before you came over?"

Vaz laughed, but in a sad sort of way. "Hey, that was a *joke*, wasn't it?" He sat down next to her. "Let's think about it for a minute. There was lipstick. The freaky breathing. And your books moving around, right? And the phone calls. Anything else?"

Lily yanked the elastic from her hair, spilling the red waves down her back. "A doll that was in the basement somehow ended up on my bed. Weird stuff in the fridge. Cold spots. Somebody filled my shoes with jam."

"That's one I haven't heard before," said Vaz.

She dragged her fingers through the snarled strands of hair. "But that doesn't mean that it was a ghost, right? I mean, it definitely wasn't."

Vaz gingerly touched the tip of his nose. "My dad talks to me sometimes."

"Hmmm," Lily said. She had something . . . *panting* in her house. Why the heck was Vaz talking about his dad?

"My dad is dead."

Lily couldn't believe what she was hearing. "What?"

"He died in a storm just off the coast six years ago. He went out fishing, and he didn't come back. They found his boat bobbing on the water. They never found his body."

"Jeez. I didn't . . . I'm sorry."

"Yeah, well." Vaz shoved his hands into his pockets. "Anyway, he talks to me sometimes."

Lily felt a pang in her gut. "What do you mean, talks?"

"I don't know. All of a sudden his voice is just . . . there, like he's right next to me. Like you are. Like the breathing in the kitchen just now. It's almost like he never left, except that he can't hear me."

"What does he say?"

"He talks about fish, mostly. The right bait you use to catch bass. The best place to find sharks and stripers. Sometimes he talks about the water. How the spray feels on your face. The sun shining white on the wake." Vaz zipped up his sweatshirt. "And then sometimes he talks about my mom. He loved my mom a lot."

Lily had a sudden dim and grainy memory of her own father, strumming the guitar, singing low and sweet with her mother looking on, and something inside Lily's throat lurched. "That's good," Lily said, before thinking about it, before stopping herself. "That's nice that he tells you."

"It's like . . . nah, forget it."

"What?"

"It's like he's been boiled down to the most essential parts of himself, you know? The most important parts are all that's left. The sea, my mom, and me." Vaz plucked at the folds in his jeans. "You think I'm crazy, right?"

She did, sort of. "Yes. No. I don't know."

"Yeah, you do. I used to think I was. I'm not, though."

"Okay."

Vaz turned to look at the house behind them, then back to her. "Let's pretend you don't think I'm crazy. Who do you think the ghost is? Who died here?"

Immediately Lily thought of Uncle Max glowing green and nuclear in the closet. "Max," she said finally.

"Who's Max?"

"My mom's uncle Max."

"How many uncles do you have?"

"There was a creepy painting of him in the front room," said Lily, ignoring his comment. "I took it down and hid it in the closet, because I didn't want to look at it. Mom said he was dead."

"Did you ask your mom how he died?"

"Yeah. But I don't think she wants to talk about it. As a matter of fact, I'm sure she doesn't want to."

Vaz tugged at the funny curl on his forehead. "Look, to get rid of the ghost, we have to figure out what he wants."

"How do we do that?"

Vaz stood. "Your favorite thing. We start reading."

Hoodlums

t he woman dug around in her voluminous straw bag with the energy and determination of a squirrel. "Where is it? I know it's in here somewhere." The flowers on her cap helicoptered furiously, as if they were attempting to lift her off the ground.

The man was lying flat on his back, towel over his face, the white belly like a great heap of bread dough. She poked him in the gut until he threw the towel aside.

"Can't a guy get a little sun around here without somebody pestering him every minute?" he shouted.

"There's no need to yell," said his wife.

"What the heck are you digging for? That scratching sound is driving me nuts."

"My book. Where's my book?"

"How should I know?"

The woman dug around some more, then snapped the bag shut in disgust. "Nothing is going right today."

"Oh, quit complaining. You can buy another book."

"That's not what I mean. Did you hear what that little hoodlum said to me?"

"Which hoodlum?"

"The one in the short skirt. She told me that I was dead, that's what she said. I think she was threatening to kill me."

"Keep your shirt on. Nobody's going to kill anyone else."

"Well, I don't like it," she said. "Kids today have no respect."

"You're right about that," he said.

"There's something wrong with that girl," the woman said. "She's up to no good. I can feel it."

"Just as long as she bothers somebody else."

"And then you knocked over that other girl's sand castle and made her cry," the woman continued.

He propped himself up on his elbows. "Aw, will you get over the sand castle already? If you have to talk, talk about the weather. Talk about . . ."

He trailed off as another man, about twenty-five, shambled in front of their beach blanket, a black, pony-sized dog with dinosaur fangs nipping playfully at his heels. "He's harmless," the man gurgled. "A sweetie. I don't know what everyone's so worried about." One side of his neck looked like beef casserole.

Husband and wife stayed completely still and silent as the man and dog shuffled away, following the figures with their eyes until the man and saber-toothed dog were out of biting range.

The woman grabbed for her purse. "I don't know what the world's coming to. I truly don't. Hoodlums. Dangerous animals roaming free. I just wish I had my book to distract myself. I know I packed it."

The man grabbed his towel and dropped it on his face. "Yeah, sure," he said, voice muffled. "Just like you packed the lemonade."

"Maybe the concession stand is open," the woman said hopefully.

"Don't hold your breath."

Chapter 10

"I hate the library," Lily grumbled.

"Quit yer bellyaching," said Vaz out of the corner of his mouth, like a cartoon pirate. She didn't complain again, since he had gone back into the house to get their coats.

The library was a tiny yellow building on a patch of crispy brown grass. Inside, the librarian sat by herself behind a large counter, frowning at an index card. Her nameplate said A. REEDY.

"Hi, Ms. Reedy," Vaz said.

The librarian was the kind of woman Lily's mother would have called handsome. She had a square, strong-featured face; iron gray hair cut in a severe wedge; lean, powerful shoulders. She had tried to soften her look with a pretty neckerchief, but it was like trying to decorate a dam with a daisy.

"Good afternoon, Vasilios," said Ms. Reedy. "You didn't finish all those books already, did you?"

"No, I'm still working on them."

"That's just fine. Just make sure you have them back on time." She tapped the card that seemed to have perturbed her so. Lily saw that it was one of the cards from the pocket of a library book and that the date stamped in red had already come and gone. "Ten cents a day for every day that a book is late," said Ms. Reedy. "It doesn't sound like much, but it adds up."

"I know. I'll return everything on time," said Vaz. He curved his mouth into a smile designed to charm testy librarians and everybody else. "I always do."

Ms. Reedy melted a bit. "Yes, I suppose you do, don't you?" She stood and placed her palms on top of the counter. "What can I do for you today?"

"My friend and I are working on a research project for school. We're studying the history of Cape May."

"We have some wonderful books that talk all about the founding of Cape May, how it began as a shore resort for wealthy Philadelphians way back in the 1600s. The city was so hot and crowded and dirty in the summer. Those poor people were looking for a little relief." Ms. Reedy's tone and expression said that she believed that cities were still as hot and crowded and dirty now as they were more than three hundred years ago. "Did you know that privateers once patrolled the coast, searching for ships to plunder and places to hide?"

"We're interested in more recent history, Ms. Reedy. The twentieth century?"

Ms. Reedy blinked. "The twentieth century?" It didn't seem to be her favorite century.

"We're interested in some of the families that lived around here. What they were up to."

"What they were up to," Ms. Reedy parroted, and frowned again, clearly wondering what *Vaz* was up to. She turned to Lily. "I don't believe I've met you before.

Are you a new student?"

"This is Lily . . . Lily—"

"Crabtree," said Lily. "I just came to town a few weeks ago."

Ms. Reedy's gold-brown eyes searched Lily's face and hair. "Crabtree? I don't suppose you could be related to the Wood family?"

"Uh . . ." said Lily. "Um . . ."

Vaz grabbed her arm, pulling her away from the desk. "Excuse us a minute, Ms. Reedy." He leaned in and whispered, "Don't tell me you don't know your family's last name."

"My mom doesn't like to talk about her family, okay? And I never asked. All I know is our last name. My mother never changed hers. She was born Arden Crabtree and she stayed Arden Crabtree."

Vaz shook his head. "*Arden* Crabtree? What is it with rich people and their funny names?"

"Look, just because my uncle has money doesn't mean that he gives us any." *And just because he offers us money doesn't mean my mom will take it.*

"Vasilios," said Ms. Reedy. "I'm sure I can help you if you tell me what it is you need to find."

"Well, Lily just moved in here, like she said, and she's staying at her uncle's on Perry Street—"

"206 Perry?" said the librarian sharply.

"Yes," said Lily. "How did you know?"

"206 Perry *is* the Wood house. I had heard that the Wood daughter married a Crabtree."

"Lily wants to research her family. We thought you might

have some newspapers that we could look through," Vaz said. "Unless you already know something about them."

Ms. Reedy grabbed both ends of the kerchief she wore and tightened it with a tug. "There are many, many families in Cape May, Vasilios. Why would you think I knew something about one of them?"

"Because you know everything about everyone," said Vaz, grinning.

Ms. Reedy smiled with half her mouth. "That makes me sound like a gossip columnist." She pulled out a stack of cards and began stamping them with the date. "I have some newspapers on microfilm that might intrigue you." *Stamp.* "If you give me some dates, I can fetch them for you." *Stamp. Stamp.*

Vaz looked at Lily, and she shrugged. "Why don't we start around 1900?" he said. "Do you have stuff going that far back?"

"Of course we do, Vasilios," said Ms. Reedy. "You wait right here and I'll get the reels from the back."

"*Vasilios?*" Lily whispered.

"Something wrong with Vasilios?"

"No," said Lily, grinning. "It's just that it sounds like something you use to treat diaper rash."

"Sorry to hear that you're still having that problem."

Lily shocked herself by whacking him in the arm and smiled when he whacked her back. It was amazing to her that she could be scared out of her wits and having fun at the same time. Maybe guys did that to you, made everything else seem smaller. Maybe that's why her mother just kept going back for more.

"Here you are. I've got issues of *The Star and Wave* from 1907 to 1970. Will that do for now?"

"Yes, thanks, Ms. Reedy."

"You be careful with that machine," Ms. Reedy said, pointing at the sole microfilm machine on a table in the corner. "It's been repaired so many times that I'm not sure it could survive another day at the shop."

Vaz nodded solemnly and took the small reels of microfilm. They sat down at the machine and turned it on. It whirred to life, sounding a lot like the propeller of an airplane.

"High tech," said Vaz as he threaded the film through the machine.

"What are we going to look for?" Lily asked.

"Any mention of your family. We can start with what we know. What's your grandfather's full name? Your mother's father? You know that, right?"

"Richard. Richard Crabtree. He died a few years ago."

"Sorry," said Vaz.

"It's okay. I didn't know him."

"Do you know how old he was when he died?"

"My mom always talks about how young he was, but I think he was in his late fifties."

"Maybe we can find a marriage announcement or something. Let's say your grandfather was close to sixty when he died. That would put his birthday around 1940. Add twenty-something years and we're talking a marriage in the 1960s sometime." He removed the reel from the machine, then searched around in the pile for the reel dated 1960. He threaded that one through the machine and turned it on. The issues whizzed by, and Vaz quickly scanned each page before Lily had time to focus. Just looking at the screen made her dizzy.

They finally found the notice in an issue dated February 12, 1963.

> Mr. and Mrs. Joseph Wood of Philadelphia are pleased to announce the engagement of their daughter, Ruth Ann, to Mr. Richard Crabtree, son of Mr. and Mrs. Harold Crabtree of New York City. The groom is a tax attorney with the firm Grandin and Pert. The bride's father is involved with a number of successful ventures, including steel, oil, and textiles. A June wedding is planned.

Lily felt strange reading about these strangers, her family. Like she should feel something more than just curiosity. She sniffed. "Mrs. Joseph Wood. Mrs. Harold Crabtree. What happened to the women's names? And here, they talk about what the groom and the bride's *father* did for a living. What about the bride? Did brides just sit around eating bonbons and looking cute? I don't think so."

"That's just how they wrote these things back then."

"No, that's how they *lived* back then. Not so different from how we live now."

Vaz held up a palm. "Peace, okay? Girl power and all that."

Ms. Reedy shelved several books in the bookcase near the reader. "How are you two doing? Can I get you anything else?"

"We're fine, Ms. Reedy. Thanks," said Vaz.

"Vaz!" said a voice behind them. "I thought that was you!"

They turned as a very blond girl ran up to them, dragging a backpack behind her. Lily recognized her as the girl Vaz had been wrestling with on the boardwalk just a few weeks before. At the sight of her, Vaz sat taller in his seat.

"Kami, please don't drag your bag on the floor," said Ms. Reedy.

"Sorry!" the girl said. To Vaz, she said, "Hey!"

"Hi, Kam. What's up?"

"Not much." She smiled at Lily. She had beautiful rosy skin and wide blue eyes. "I'm Kami."

"Lily." Lily could see a silver hoop threaded through the cartilage at the top of Kami's ear.

"Lily just moved here," said Vaz.

"You poor thing," Kami said, half smiling, half grimacing. "Unless you're into Victorian house tours you're going to be pretty bored till summer." She unwound one of the five knit scarves she wore. "How's the nose?"

"It hasn't fallen off yet," Vaz said.

"Yet," said Kami, squinting her eyes up in a way that Lily assumed was supposed to be cute. Kami reached out and touched the tip of Vaz's nose with a glittery fingernail. "We may have to glue it on to be sure."

Vaz grinned even wider.

Kami waggled frayed ends of her purple scarf. "Listen, I can't hang around, my mom wants me home early today, but maybe we can hang out tomorrow or over the weekend? J. D. might be having a party."

"Sure. I'll call you."

"Cool!" She tossed the end of her scarf around her neck as if she were Amelia Earhart off to fly the world. "Great meeting you, Lily."

"Yeah," said Lily. "Great."

Kami flounced away, dragging her backpack behind her.

"She seems nice," said Lily. *If you like hip, gorgeous blondes.*

Vaz's eyes followed Kami out the door. "Yeah, Kami's the best."

Lily watched him watch Kami and worried that he would start barking and drooling. "So where were we?" she said, swallowing a knot of disappointment that had risen in her throat.

"Why don't we go back a ways and see if there's anything in here about the Woods or your uncle's house?"

"My mom said the house has been in the family for a hundred years."

They removed the 1960s reel and threaded the machine with the first reel, which covered issues from 1907 to 1910. They scanned articles until their eyes nearly crossed, but found no mention of the Woods or the house on Perry Street. They quickly moved on to the 1910 reel. No luck there, either.

Ms. Reedy hovered behind them. "You are being careful with that machine?"

"Absolutely," said Vaz.

Ms. Reedy looked at the screen. "Finding anything interesting?"

"We found a marriage announcement, but not much else," said Lily.

"Keep looking," she said. "A good researcher is always persistent." She walked back to the front desk.

"I don't know how persistent I want to be," said Lily. "This is making me nauseous."

Vaz threaded the machine with the 1920s reel. He cranked the knob on the machine and tried to focus the picture. The film was blank. The entire reel was blank.

"Try the next reel," said Lily.

They tried the 1930s reel, but it looked as if nothing had ever been recorded on it at all.

"This is too weird," Vaz said.

Lily closed her eyes. "You're telling me. Try the last one."

Vaz removed the 1930s reel and replaced it with the 1940s reel. He whizzed through the reel, but all they saw on it was a couple of hairs and some particles of dust.

"Wait! Stop! Go back," said Lily. "I thought I saw something."

"What? An ant leg? A fly wing?" Vaz asked, but rolled back the reel anyway.

"There!" said Lily.

"What the heck . . ." began Vaz, but trailed off.

They stared at the screen in front of them. It looked as if someone had held a match under the film, scorching black letters into the plastic.

YOU'RE GETTING WARMER.

what goes up must come down WHAT GOES UP MUST COME DOWN what go

What Goes Up
Must Come Down

madame Durriken sat at her table, hands snatching at her fleecy hair as she pored over the tarot-card books piled all around her. Though she had read the tarot cards for customers every day, sometimes a dozen times a day, she had always been somewhat creative when divining the future with them.

In other words, she just made things up.

"'The Tower,'" she read. "'Prepare to adjust to new situations. Being irritable is not going to help.'"

"Being irritable *always* helps," said Madame Durriken, and tossed the book over her shoulder.

She hadn't opened the Good Fortunes Shoppe since she had first seen the boy with the burning hands some weeks before. Six separate times now, Madame Durriken had watched the blond woman with the orange cloak scurry down the brick walk with the leering boy prancing behind her like some demented pony.

He was clearly a sick puppy. And he had clearly seen Madame Durriken watching. Madame Durriken was determined to find out who he was and what he was up to.

Her profession notwithstanding, she didn't have any experience with ghosts, not real ones. Then again, if he was after the woman in the orange cloak, then Madame herself didn't have anything to worry about and could go back to cheating her customers as usual. But who knew what a ghost was after?

That was when she decided that it might not be a bad idea to try to read the tarot cards. *Really* read them. She'd attended many conventions with so-called psychics—kooks and screwballs with just a couple of brain cells among them—and watched them read the cards as easily as they could read a calendar. If the kooks could do it, surely a woman with Madame Durriken's brains and sensitivity could do it, too.

She pulled a deck of worn tarot cards from the pocket of her satin robe and cut the deck with her practiced hands. After taking a deep rattling breath, she laid down the first card.

Queen of Swords. Madame pulled another tarot book from the pile and read: " 'A quick-witted woman.' " Madame smiled to herself, remembering how often she had savored her own sharp wit.

She placed the second card over the first. The second card was supposed to tell her what forces were operating against her. Knight of Wands. Her eyes narrowed to slits when she saw the picture on the card, a fair young man with a fiery torch held high. The book said that this mischievous young man could be troubling.

"No kidding," said Madame Durriken.

She placed the third card beneath the first two. Three of Swords. The card depicted a red heart pierced by three long swords with black handles. Blood dripped down one of the swords.

"Pretty," said Madame Durriken, flipping through her book. "'Pain.'" She scowled. "Yeah, sure. A pain in the neck, you mean."

Shaking her head, she placed the fourth card facedown to the left of cards one and two. "You're supposed to tell me what happened in my recent past, as if I don't know."

She flipped the card. The Fool.

"Excuse me?" Madame snapped. She consulted the book. "'The beginning of a journey. At a crossroads. Choose your path wisely.'"

"What journey? What crossroads? I've lived in this lousy town for twenty years!"

She immediately slapped down the fifth card. The Eight of Swords. "'Confused, under pressure.'"

"Can we please get to the point?" The sixth card, the immediate future card, was the Two of Cups. "'A tender new romance or a beautiful friendship. A wonderful surprise.'" It sounded like the romantic twaddle her clients always begged to hear from her.

She skipped the next three cards, which were supposed to reveal her hopes and fears and what other people thought of her. (As if she needed to be told that she *hoped* she'd be rich, she *feared* she wouldn't be, and other people thought she was a genius.)

The tenth and final card, the outcome of the situation, the answer. "Come on," she said to the back of the card, doing her best to keep from yelling. "Just give me a little information? Just a hint? What's the kid want? Who's he mad at? That's all I want to know."

She turned the card over. The Wheel of Fortune. "'What goes up must come down.'"

"That's it? That's it?" shouted Madame Durriken. "I could have gotten that out of a fortune cookie!" She stood, swept the tarot cards off the table with one long, branchlike arm, and watched as they fluttered to the floor.

Twenty years she had been coming to this shop day in, day out, slaving over crystal balls and sweaty palms to give knuckle-headed tourists a little excitement. And for what? So that she could end up haunted by some demented dead kid? This was no kind of life for a person of her talent and intelligence. She should have bought into those condos in South Carolina when she had the chance. Now she was stuck.

She looked down at the table. A single tarot card, facedown, remained on its surface. *Why not?* she thought, and turned it over.

A creature with a man's torso, furred haunches and cloven feet. Horns curling madly from a high forehead. A sly smirk. Men and women, small and cowed as rabbits, chained at his side.

The Devil.

"Pure hokum," warbled Madame Durriken with a reedy note of fear in her voice. She stood and kicked at the cards piled on the floor, flipping a few of them faceup. The horned man smirked at her from each.

"What?" she cried, her bony hands pressed to her sunken cheeks. "That's impossible! There's only one in the deck!"

She dropped to her knees and frantically flipped the cards. The Devil. The Devil. The Devil. The Devil. All of them, every single one.

Chapter 11

"I'm sorry to have to tell you this, Ms. Reedy," said Vaz, stacking the microfilm on the counter in front of the librarian. "But these reels are blank. Mostly. And one of them was . . . messed up a little."

The frown lines around Ms. Reedy's mouth deepened. "What do you mean, blank? Messed up?"

"There isn't anything on them," said Lily.

"That's impossible," said Ms. Reedy.

"You can check for yourself," said Vaz.

Ms. Reedy's mouth got so tight, her lips vanished. "I can't believe it," she said. "I don't know how many times I tell people that they must treat library materials respectfully, but do they listen? No. They just do whatever they please, with no regard for—"

"Ms. Reedy, um, excuse me, but do you have any other copies of these newspapers anywhere? Maybe in the back room?"

Ms. Reedy opened each reel of microfilm and peered into the case. "I'm afraid to say that I do not have other copies of these materials."

Vaz tapped the counter lightly with a pencil. "Do you know where else we can find newspapers like these? In another branch of the library, maybe?"

"There is a branch in Cape May Court House. About twelve miles up Route Nine. I'm not sure if there's bus service. Perhaps one of your parents can take you?"

Vaz put his elbows on the counter and leaned forward. "There's nowhere else you can look? No secret papers in the basement that only you know about?"

Ms. Reedy drew back. "Secret papers? Vasilios, I think you've been watching too many movies!"

"Reading too many books, you mean," Vaz said, and pulled his elbows from the counter. "Thanks anyway, Ms. Reedy."

Vaz and Lily were almost out the door when Ms. Reedy said, "Wait a moment!"

They walked back to the counter. "I suppose I do have some books that might be helpful."

"That would be great, Ms. Reedy."

"And, and . . ." Ms. Reedy tugged on the ends of her scarf. "You *could* contact Bailey Burton at the Historical Association. I'm sure *its* library is well stocked with books and papers you can use." She sniffed. "The Historical Association has many generous benefactors."

"Where is the Historical Association, Ms. Reedy?" Lily asked.

The librarian looked at Lily. "Bailey Burton runs the Historical Association from his home. On Perry Street. Number 204."

"That's right next door to your house," Vaz said as they walked out of the building.

"Yeah, I know. And I think my uncle knows that

Burton guy, too. We had to get the house keys from him when we first got here."

"He probably knows all about the house, then," said Vaz. "We won't have to read any more microfilm."

"Maybe," said Lily, thinking about Bailey Burton, aka Angry Baby Man. "He wasn't all that friendly."

Vaz handed Lily the three books on Cape May they had taken out and looked at his watch. "It's almost five o'clock. We probably won't have time to go talk to that Historical Association guy today, but maybe we can go tomorrow? I can come over after school."

Out of the corner of her eye, she watched Vaz walking alongside her, his stride long and confident. She liked him, but what did she know about him? What about super-blond, super-cute, super-cool Kami? Would he change his mind if Kami wanted him to come over?

"Hello?" Vaz poked her in the arm. "Is tomorrow okay or not?"

"Sorry, I was just thinking. Yeah, tomorrow's fine."

"Are you sure?"

"Sure," Lily said, not sure at all.

"Why are you looking at me like that?" Vaz asked.

"Like what?"

"Like I have some kind of gunk caught in my teeth and you don't want to tell me."

Skin hot, Lily turned her face away. "I was just thinking that I should go to meet my mom at the store. It's in the mall. I don't want something I can't see breathing on me again."

They took the long way from the library to the mall,

weaving through the city, meandering past rows and rows of elaborately painted houses even larger and fancier than Uncle Wes's. A few had placards hanging from their mailboxes with names like The Jeremiah Hand House and The Abbey in curlicues and flowers. Vaz saw her staring.

"There are plenty of regular houses in this town that don't look like that," he said. "All you have to do is work your way back from the shore, go north a little bit, and you'll see what I mean."

"Where do you live?" Lily asked.

"North," he said, one corner of his mouth turned up. "In a little house about, um, ten blocks that way. Pretty far."

"I used to walk thirty or forty blocks sometimes, when I lived in New York City."

His eyes widened at the words *New York*. "I've never been to New York City. What was it like to live there?"

"Okay. Lots of really cool museums, like the American Museum of Natural History. But my mom worked a lot. New York is expensive."

"And it was just you and your mom?"

"When we first moved there, there was a guy. Some political activist or something. He was nice, but kinda dull, always going on and on about the government and the capitalists. My mom thought they would move in together and maybe get married someday. But that guy decided he didn't want to be so active anymore and moved to Seattle to open up a coffee shop. So it was just us. And Julep. My cat."

"So where else have you lived?"

"Well, I was born in California. We lived there until I was five. Then we moved to Chicago. Then it was Indianapolis, then Cleveland Heights in Ohio; Pittsburgh, Pennsylvania; and then New York City. After that, New Jersey—Hoboken, Jersey City, Wayne. We ended up in Montclair. And now, here."

"You moved ten times in eight years?"

"Three of those were in the same year."

Vaz whistled. "You guys really get around."

"It's not like I wanted to," Lily said.

"Maybe not, but it sounds kind of cool to me." Vaz glanced down at her. "How long do you think you'll stay here?"

"I don't know. Summertime, probably. Or until my mom meets another one of her frogs—oh, I mean Prince Charmings."

Vaz smiled but didn't comment. "Here's the mall," he said. "Looks weird in the winter. Nobody here. You should see how packed this place gets in the summer. Shoobies everywhere."

"Shoobies? What's a shoobie?"

"Tourists."

"Why do you call them shoobies?"

"I figured you'd ask that," Vaz said. "Back in the 1800s, poor people who came to the shore just for the day would bring their lunches in shoeboxes. The rich people got annoyed that their fancy hotels were being overrun with 'those kinds of people' and called them shoobies. It kind of stuck. Now that you live here, you'll have to start using the correct terminology."

"I'll try to remember that."

He gave her a long look. "Did you know that your eyes

look exactly like green olives?" he asked. "Without the pimientos, of course."

"No, I guess I didn't." Lily said. Did Vaz *like* olives? "Um . . . um. . . ," she stammered, "here's my mom's store. I mean, I hope this is it. I don't think there are two stores named Something Fishy." Lily caught her tongue between her teeth to stop herself from babbling.

The door to the jewelry shop flew open, and Lily's mother peeked out. "I thought I saw you through the window," she said. "What are you doing out in the cold?" She grinned at Vaz, who smiled back.

Lily had no choice but to introduce him. "Mom, this is Vaz. Vaz, this is my mom."

"Hello, Mrs. Crabtree. Nice to meet you," he said.

"Ms. It's *Ms*. Crabtree. And it's *wonderful* to meet you!" she said, and winked.

Lily shoved her hands into her pockets. She hated when her mother winked.

"So, Lily, I'll see you tomorrow?" Vaz said.

"Yeah, okay," she mumbled.

"Bye," he said.

As soon as he was out of earshot, Lily's mother said, "Where'd you find the hot taco?"

Lily pushed her mother into the store. "The hot *what*?"

Lily's mother backed up and shut the door, the bells that hung from it rattling. "Hot taco. He looks like a spicy one. Don't you think so?"

Any guy her mother liked was guaranteed to be a complete fraud. Lily's heart thumped. "I don't think of guys as food products, Mom." Lily dropped the books on the floor and unzipped her coat, almost ripping off her finger-nail in the process. "And you shouldn't talk like that."

"Like what?"

"About hot tacos. It's not normal."

Lily's mother hiked up her acid green skirt around her pink-stockinged calves like a flamenco dancer. "You were expecting normal? Since when?"

"Never mind."

Lily's mother dropped her skirt. "Are you wearing lip-stick?"

Lily wiped a hand across her lips. "It's juice."

"Juice?"

"Juice," Lily said. "So are you going to show me around or not?"

"Are you going to tell me about Dark and Handsome?"

"Nope."

"So I might as well show you around."

True to its name, the store was packed with jewelry and gifts inspired by the ocean and its residents. Lots of shell brooches and necklaces, vases encrusted with coral, lamp shades made of beach glass. Lily poked at a pair of earrings shaped like tiny little women in bikinis. The polka-dotted bottoms were loose and wriggled if you flicked them.

Lily's mother wrinkled her nose. "I refuse to take responsibility for that. Not my work."

"Yeah, I know," said Lily. "You're usually not this cheesy."

"*Usually?*" Lily's mother said. "I seem to remember a certain little girl who loved my work. You even wanted to make jewelry yourself, remember?"

"Not really."

"Oh, sure you do. You were always stealing my pliers. Do you want to see what I'm working on now?"

Lily sighed. "All right."

Lily's mother circled the glass counter, packed with bracelets, rings, and watches, and slipped into the back room. She returned with a little blue velvet pouch, which she handed to Lily.

"What's this?" Lily asked.

"Open it."

Lily slipped a pinkie into the top of the pouch, loosening the drawstring. She turned the open pouch, and a thin silver chain with a round pendant slid into her waiting palm.

"Wow, Mom," said Lily, inspecting the battered silver pendant.

"This is what Julep was whacking around the night that Uncle Wes came over. I found it under the couch. I had to solder a link for the chain, but other than that, it was perfect the way I found it."

The light winked off the pendant's funky raised markings. "What are these symbols?"

"I don't know. You can't really make them out, can you?"

"I like how it's all beaten up." Lily held the necklace out to her mother. "Really nice work. How much are you going to charge for it?"

"Nothing," Lily's mother said. "It's a gift. For you."

"Mom, you can get at least a hundred dollars for this, I know it"—but as she spoke Lily turned to the mirror sitting on the countertop to see what the necklace would look like hanging from her neck. The pendant fit perfectly in the hollow between her collarbones.

Her mother appeared in the mirror behind her. "Now how can I sell it after I've seen how gorgeous it looks on you?"

"But, Mom—"

"Really, Lily, I made it for you. I want you to have it. Please." Her mother put both hands on Lily's shoulders and squeezed.

Lily was about to argue some more but saw the pleading look on her mother's face. She fingered the pendant. "It *is* pretty cool."

Her mother beamed. "I knew you'd like it." She kissed Lily's cheek. "I'm starved. What do you say we pick up some things for dinner and go home?"

Lily helped her mother put her tools away in the back room. They put on their scarves and coats and turned off all the lights. They were locking up the store when Lily's mother leaned over and whispered in Lily's ear. "Don't look now, but that odd woman from across the street is spying on us. I said don't look!"

But Lily had already turned and caught the woman staring out at them from her store window. She looked like a badly drawn stick figure in a gray fur hat. She immediately ducked out of sight behind a heavy black drape.

"The Good Fortunes Shoppe," said Lily, pronouncing the last word *shoppy*.

"I think it's pronounced *shop*, Lily," her mother told her.

"Shop, shoppy, whatever." Lily read the list of services

etched onto the glass in the door. TAROT, PALM, AND PSYCHIC READINGS. MEDIUM SERVICES AVAILABLE BY APPOINTMENT. "What's a medium?"

"Somebody who thinks they can talk to ghosts."

"Ghosts?" Lily said, biting her lip.

"Yup."

They walked for a few minutes in silence.

"Do you believe in them, Mom?"

"Do I believe in what?"

"Ghosts."

Her mother's face was suddenly grim as a headstone. "Only the live ones."

Chapter 12

Lily hadn't known what to expect when she and her mother came home from the grocery store, but it wasn't what she found.

The house, which had seemed so frightening and bizarre when she and Vaz had been chased out of it, was suddenly as quiet and ordinary as any on Perry Street, as any anywhere. There were no objects flapping around, no invisible beings hyperventilating, no spirits or thieves marching up and down the stairs or crouching in the toilets. The phone sat as unruffled as a cat. And, as for the cat herself, she was snoozing on top of the refrigerator.

That's it, Lily thought. *I'm losing my mind.*

Lily's mother put a pot of water on the stove to boil the hot dogs they'd bought. "Thanks for cleaning up," she said dryly, picking up a spoon that had been pasted to the countertop with peanut sauce.

"Sorry, Mom. We had to leave in a hurry."

"We?" said her mother. "This wouldn't be you and the hot taco, now would it?"

"Um . . ."

Lily's mother pulled some buns from the plastic grocery bag. "Look, I'm thrilled that you're making friends and all that, but I'm not so thrilled with the idea of you having boys over when I'm not here."

"He just came by for a little while." Lily debated telling her mother about the phone call and the breathing but remembered her mother's you're-just-making-things-up-because-you're-mad attitude. "We just had some Thai food and talked about *The Old Man and the Sea*."

"Uh-huh."

"It's true!" Lily took the spoon from her mother's hand. "I mean, look who you're talking to. What do you think I'm going to do? Have all my junior-high friends over for a rave?"

Lily's mother laughed. "I guess that's highly unlikely. Still—"

"Come on, Mom. He said he was going to come over tomorrow and help me with the stupid book. He *likes* that book."

"Really? He likes *The Old Man and the Sea*?"

"Yes," said Lily. "But I've decided not to hold it against him."

"Big of you," her mother said. "Did you finish those essay questions?"

"Um . . ."

"Um yourself. Tomorrow's your last chance, okay? Otherwise I'm going to make you wade through *Moby Dick*. Get it? Wade?"

Lily covered her ears. "Bad, Mom. That was really bad."

Lily was sure that the nightfall would bring more surprises, or at least a little uneasiness, but the quiet of the house and her mother's presence lulled her into questioning that anything *really* scary had happened there at all.

By the time Lily was perched at her usual spot at the dining-room table the next day, she had convinced herself that if there was a ghost or a spy, he didn't know who he was dealing with.

At age nine, she had fed Julep through a dropper for twenty days after discovering the four-week-old kitten in a garbage can on Mott Street in New York City. At ten, she was baby-sitting for the family in the apartment next door. At eleven, she had driven her mother to the hospital when bad chicken had made her mother too sick to handle the car. Lily had taken care of herself since she was little, since the terrible night her father had taken his guitar to a gig and hadn't bothered to come back.

She wasn't going to scare so easily.

At three thirty the next afternoon, Vaz showed up with a box of hot chocolate. "My turn to buy," he said. "Maybe we can have some after we talk to the Bailey guy?" He said this as if a cup of hot chocolate in Lily's kitchen were a date at a nice restaurant. Lily's toes curled inside her worn boots.

"Okay," Lily said shyly, taking the box and putting it on the floor by the stairs. "Maybe we'll even be able to drink it without somebody breathing all over us."

Lily got her coat, and she and Vaz walked next door to Bailey Burton's house. Bright red with blue-and-white trim and little stars cut into the woodwork above the porch, the house looked like a giant, three-dimensional flag. Lily rang the bell and stuffed her hand back into her pocket to keep it warm.

The door opened a crack and a lone raisin eye glared at

them. "What is it? Who are you? What do you want?" He sprayed these questions like a man who wouldn't ever be satisfied with the answers to them.

"Hello again, Mr. Burton. Remember me? Me and my mother are staying—"

"My mother and I," barked the man.

"Excuse me?"

"It's not *me and my mother*. It's *my mother and I*."

"Oh. Well," said Lily, sneaking a confused glance at Vaz. "My mother and I are staying at the house next door?"

"Don't ask a question if you're making a statement. It makes you sound like an ignoramus."

Lily squared her shoulders, getting irritated with the raisin and with the person it belonged to. "My mother and I are staying at the house next door. It's my uncle Wes's house. The librarian told us that you run the Historical Association."

"*She* sent you? What for?"

Vaz and Lily looked at each other. "She thought you could help us," said Lily.

"With what?"

"Since you know my uncle, I was wondering if you knew anything about the house or maybe could help us figure out some of the history of the house."

The door opened wider to accommodate the man's other eye, but not so wide that Lily and Vaz could see the man's whole face, just a stripe down the middle. The piggy eyes looked like chips dropped in pancake batter.

"I don't know what that woman was thinking when she sent you here, but I'm sure that your uncle would be happy to tell you the history of the house. If he knows what it is. Why don't you ask him?"

"Well, um, it's a surprise," Lily said. "I thought I would do a family tree for my uncle. As a present. For letting us stay at his house."

The man's smile was cold and empty as a snowman's. "I'd love to help you, but I'm afraid that your uncle's house, your uncle's family, are a bit of a mystery. Not a lot of records on them."

"Excuse me, sir," Vaz said, stepping forward, "but we were hoping that you might have some copies of some old newspapers or pictures. Maybe there's something you missed."

The piggy eyes pinned Vaz. "I don't miss much. If there was something about that house to be found in the Historical Association's library, I would have found it already." The man drew himself up to his less-than-considerable height. "I am the foremost authority on Cape May history in this area. As a matter of fact, I wrote two books on the subject."

"That's very nice, but—"

"I don't think I can help you," the man interrupted.

"Maybe we can just see the library—"

"The library is closed for the time being. I'm packing things up in order to move it to a new location in a few weeks, and most of the documents are already in boxes. I'm sorry."

He didn't sound sorry. Vaz said, "But—"

The man tipped his egglike head. "What are you?"

"Excuse me?"

"You're awfully dark. What are you?"

Vaz turned darker, dark red. "I'm Greek."

"Greek?" said the man, and slammed the door shut.

They stood there in shock for several minutes, until Vaz turned abruptly and marched down the stairs. Lily had to scamper to keep up with him.

"That guy. . . ," Vaz spit.

Lily nodded in agreement, but Vaz wasn't even looking. His face had turned a deep shade of plum.

"Forget him, Vaz. He's just a little man with a complex."

"He's not alone, you know. There's a lot of people just like him in this town."

"There's a lot of people like him everywhere, Vaz. The worst thing is to let them get to you."

"That's easy for you to say."

Lily felt as if she'd been punched in the stomach. "What are you talking about? What do you mean?"

Vaz scuffed his sneakers on the sidewalk. "Forget it."

"You think I don't know what it's like to have people hate me for no reason? Did you ever try to go to school in a ritzy neighborhood in clothes from the Salvation Army?"

"Look, you're right," he said, running a hand through his hair. "It's just that it's the second time it happened to me this month."

"The second time?"

Vaz touched the tip of his nose. "Remember this? There's a kid who'll call you a spick and a greaser if you've got more pigment than the moon. Most of the time nobody pays any attention to him. But this last time I couldn't help it."

"Uh-oh."

"He couldn't bother me, so he decided to bother my mom at work. She's a waitress at Gorgeous George's Crab House. He went there with a couple of his friends, requested a table in her section, then called her a wetback, a greaser, and everything else their feeble little minds could think up. Her hair is red!" he said, as if that made a difference. "Then they stiffed her for the bill." Vaz was plumming up again. "The manager is just as bad as the kids. He made her pay for that bill."

"But that's not fair," said Lily.

"Tell me about it. So I jumped the guy after school. He broke my nose."

Lily winced. "Maybe you should just have started a rumor that he wears girl's underwear or something."

"Hey, that's pretty good," said Vaz, "but it worked out okay. I picked his pocket while he was pounding on me. He had twenty-two bucks and a pack of gum. I gave my mom the money. I gave the gum to my dog. His name's Argos. Isn't that a cool name?"

"Argos?"

"Odysseus's dog? The one who lived more than twenty years and then died when Odysseus finally came back?"

"Oh, *that* Argos."

"Lily, you really have to start reading some books, girl."

She stood in the doorway, watching her breath cotton up the air in front of her, wondering why he would stand in the cold and fight with her, what he wanted. Then she thought about what she wanted. She wanted to know what was going on. She wanted to stop being the serious girl whose wacky mother had more boyfriends and more fun.

She grabbed his sleeve and hauled him into the house and shut the door behind him.

"My mom told me about chicks like you."

"I didn't want that guy to hear us talking," Lily said. She scooped up the box of hot chocolate, unzipped her coat, and led him into the kitchen. "I think we've got to get a look at that library."

"But the guy just told us that it's closed. He's packing it up to move it."

"Come on. Something weird's going on. Did you hear what he said? 'I don't know what *that woman* was thinking when she sent you here.'"

"Yeah? So?"

"So did you really believe that he's packing his archive to move it?"

Vaz smiled wryly. "No. I don't think Mr. You're Awfully Dark What Are You wants to help us."

Lily pulled a packet of hot chocolate from the box. "That's why we're going to help ourselves."

"What do you suggest?"

She tore off the top of the packet with her teeth, surprising herself for once. "How do you feel about a little breaking and entering?"

Chapter 13

Lily and Vaz agreed to watch Bailey Burton's house for a couple of days before they tried to do anything against the law.

"We'll keep track of when he comes and goes, and how long he's gone," said Lily. "That way we'll know the best time for us to break in."

Vaz eyed her with what she hoped was admiration. "Are you sure you haven't done this before?"

He and Lily did most of the spying together, running from one window to the next, peering out, making notes in a notebook.

"Duck!" Vaz dived beneath the window, pulling Lily down with him.

"What's going on?" Lily asked.

"Burton was looking right into this window. I think he saw us."

"So?"

"So you have *binoculars* around your neck, Lily."

Lily looked down, first at the binoculars, then at Vaz's hand still holding hers. "So maybe we're bird-watching or something."

"Come on."

She sat up and leaned against the wall. "Look. He's been

going out at three every afternoon and coming back around five. What do you think about trying it then?"

"Kind of risky," said Vaz. "It's the middle of the day."

"Most people are still at work. And we'll try the basement windows in the back of the house. The ones behind the bushes. Even if someone were looking, they wouldn't see us."

"Good idea," said Vaz, leaning up against the wall next to her. "You know, you may have a future in crime."

Lily pulled the binoculars over her head. "I have a future in engineering."

"Is that what you want to be?"

"That or an accountant. Or maybe something else in finance. Whatever pays the best. I like science, but they don't pay scientists very well. My mom might think being poor is cool, but I don't."

"Finance," said Vaz. "I'm impressed. I have no idea what I'm going to do. I don't want to work in a restaurant. And I don't want to be a fisherman. Did you know that being a fisherman is more dangerous than being a cop?"

She remembered his father, the empty boat bobbing on the water. "I didn't know that."

"Well, it's true."

"Has your father . . . um . . . said anything about that?"

"You mean is my dead dad giving me career advice when he haunts me?"

"Yeah," she said. "I guess that's what I mean." Lily was surprised he could speak so matter-of-factly about his father, about his *ghost* father. She didn't even like to mention the fact that she *had* a father. "Does he ever tell you what you should do?"

"He doesn't tell me what I should do or not do, just what *he* did. And Dad loved fishing. Apart from me and my mom, it was his whole entire life. But since he died, I don't like it much." For a moment, Vaz's face went all loose and sad, but then he smiled and bumped her in the shoulder with his own. "How about we go into business together? You can be the accountant and I'll be the idea man."

"The what?"

"The idea man. You know, the guy who thinks of all the big ideas, the guy who understands the big picture."

"And what's the big picture?"

"Guys are better than girls."

"Can you get us in the house?" Lily asked.

"No."

"Then *I'll* be the idea man. We break in tomorrow."

The next day, a half hour after Bailey Burton locked up his front door, Lily and Vaz were crouched next to Bailey Burton's basement windows and were thrilled to find that he kept them unlocked. The basement was dim but not dark. Lots of boxes and old furniture lay rotting on the damp floor, and there was a strong smell of mildew.

"Ladies first," Lily said, and crawled in front of the window. She turned to face Vaz, then put both feet into the opening and wriggled her body through like a woman trying to fit into a tight pair of jeans. She landed with a soft thud on top of a pile of soggy newspapers.

"Ugh," she whispered. "I think something died down here."

Vaz wriggled through the opening feet first, the way Lily had, also landing on the newspapers. "Man!" he whispered, covering his nose. "Let's get upstairs. He wouldn't keep anything important down here. It's too . . . gross." Vaz lifted one of the newspapers, which seemed to be growing dozens of little brown feet. "Mushrooms," he said, pulling out the tiny disposable camera that he'd brought.

"What are you doing?"

"Taking a picture."

"For what?"

"Science class."

They made their way through the piles of junk, trying very hard not to touch anything, and walked up the basement stairs. The door at the top was closed, and they looked at each other as Lily turned the knob and slowly pushed open the door.

The dining-room table was worse than any dump. Half-eaten burgers were half wrapped in tissue paper and shoved into empty pizza boxes upon which cheese had hardened into plastic. Old soda cups leaked sugary water onto the scratched surface of the table. Paper plates littered with crumbs and smeared with sauces perched on every surface: the chairs, the top of the buffet, the piles of books.

"I think Mr. Burton's got an eating disorder," said Vaz.

"It's disordered, all right," said Lily. She kicked at a burger that was on the floor with a few bites taken out of it. It reminded her of a leaf ravaged by a hungry caterpillar. Lily pictured Bailey Burton and revised her label for him: he wasn't Angry Baby Man, he was Angry Larva Man.

Vaz picked up a straw and lifted the corner of a pizza box. "Do you think there are any human bones under all this?"

Lily shivered. "Let's find that stupid library before we catch something."

"Or worse."

They walked through the dining room, down the hallway. They found the library on the other side of the large front staircase. Unlike the other rooms they had seen, the library was clean and neat, dominated by several huge bookshelves, a spotless fireplace, and a large oak desk.

"I bet this is the only room he lets people see," said Lily.

"People would run screaming if they saw anything else," said Vaz. He ran a finger over the spines of all the books on the shelves. "Look at all the weird books he has." He pulled out a volume. "*The Life Cycle of the Horseshoe Crab.*"

"It's nice that he keeps up with his relatives," said Lily.

He walked a few feet and pulled out another book. "*Bold in Her Britches.*" He flipped to the back cover. "It's about girl pirates."

"That's even cooler than the crabs," said Lily.

"Not necessarily," said Vaz. "The crabs could eat the girl pirates. It's a food-chain thing."

"We found fungus in the basement and bacteria in the dining room. This whole place is a food-chain thing," said Lily. Her stomach was quivering, both in disgust and in excitement. "Do you see any newspapers or anything?"

"No, not yet."

"He's got to keep them around here somewhere. You

don't think he has them on microfilm or something, do you?"

"He could, I guess," said Vaz. "But I don't see a reader." He plucked a model of a ship off the mantel. "*Quedah Merchant*, 1699. I know this name, but I can't remember where I heard it."

"I think I found the papers," said Lily.

There was a rectangular wooden rack with rows of spokes running horizontally. A newspaper was draped over each spoke like a pair of slacks on a hanger. Lily removed a paper. "*The Star and Wave*," she read. "September 29, 2002." She put the paper back and pulled out another. "November 13, 2002." She shook her head. "These are too recent. The older ones have to be somewhere else."

Vaz put the model back on the mantel. "Did you look in all these books?" He knelt and gestured to a shelf full of large albums covered with leather. "These look like big scrapbooks or something." He sat on the floor and opened one in his lap. "This is it, Lily. Look!"

Lily sat down next to him. The large albums contained copies of old Cape May newspapers, with each paper in its own plastic cover. "He keeps his old newspapers cleaner than he keeps his silverware," she said. "What's the date on that album?"

"1977."

"Okay," said Lily. "Is there a book for 1930?" She scooted on her knees across the floor, head tilted sideways so that she could read the legends. "Yes! Here it is, 1930." She pulled it off the shelf and opened it on the floor. She and Vaz flipped through the articles.

"There's a lot on the Depression here, but not much else," said Vaz. "Let's try the next volume."

They replaced 1930 and pulled out 1931, 1932, 1933. After some reading and flipping, Lily said, "Look at this. 1934.

> Mr. and Mrs. Arthur Spicer wish to announce the marriage of their daughter, Miss Katherine Spicer, to Mr. Joseph Wood of Philadelphia. The couple plans to winter in Philadelphia and summer at the Wood family home on Perry Street in Cape May.

"Katherine Spicer and Joseph Wood! They have to be my great-grandparents!"

They removed that section of the paper out of its protective cover and snapped a picture of the marriage announcement. Then they flipped through the rest of the pages, hoping to find something else that mentioned the Spicers or the Woods or the house on Perry Street, but found nothing.

"We got dirt," said Vaz.

"Try the next one."

1935 was a good year.

> Mr. and Mrs. Joseph Wood of Philadelphia and Cape May are pleased to welcome their daughter, Ruth Ann, born in April.

They snapped another photo.

They had to look through two more volumes before they found anything else.

> Mr. and Mrs. Joseph Wood of Philadelphia and
> Cape May are pleased to welcome their son,
> Wesley Arthur, born in November.

"Keep digging," said Lily. "There's got to be something about Max next."

They found that notice in 1943.

> Mr. and Mrs. Joseph Wood of Philadelphia and
> Cape May are pleased to welcome their son,
> Maxmillian Joseph, born in July.

Lily and Vaz looked at each other. "Uncle Max," Lily said. "It's a good thing they don't have any baby pictures."

Vaz focused the camera on the birth announcement. "That scary, huh?"

She thought of the weird painting hidden away in the closet. The sickening smile. The glowing eyes. "That scary," said Lily.

Vaz looked at his watch. "We don't have much time left. Why don't we split the volumes? It will go faster."

They each paged through the big albums one by one, 1944, 1945, 1946. Lily made a discovery in 1951.

> Cape May lost one of its most prominent citizens
> this weekend. Mr. Joseph Wood died of a heart

ailment late Saturday night. He was 52 years old. A public service is planned for Wednesday.

"Your family has had some pretty bad luck," Vaz said.

"No kidding," said Lily. Joseph. Her great-grandfather. She wondered what he was like. If his family missed him after he was gone.

"Here's something interesting," said Vaz. "1955. Mysterious fire in a barn."

"I've got something about a mysterious fire in 1956, too. A boat burned up."

"Weird," said Vaz. "But that doesn't have anything to do with anything, does it?"

Lily shrugged, finished going through 1957 and 1958. "Another fire in '58," she read. "A concession stand at the beach. The police suspect that it's arson. I wonder if they ever found the guy."

"How do you know it was a guy?" said Vaz.

"Same way that I just knew you were going to say that."

"Maybe it was a gang of girl arsonists."

"They probably were in a turf war with the girl pirates."

There were no fires in 1959, and no mention of the Woods.

"I don't think that we're going to find any more here," said Vaz, "and Burton is going to be back to tend his fungus farm in about fifteen minutes."

"One more, okay?" said Lily. "We have time." She flipped open the cover of 1960 and gasped. "Vaz! Look!"

A mysterious and tragic fire erupted on the third floor of 206 Perry Street late Saturday night. One person was killed.

Owned by Mrs. Joseph Wood, the house suffered moderate fire and water damage but was saved before the fire reached the second-floor bedrooms, where most of the family were sleeping.

The deceased has been identified as Maxmillian Wood, seventeen. Investigators believe that the young man may have started the fire as a prank but was trapped on the third floor when the fire raged out of control. Memorial services are scheduled for Monday. The funeral will follow on Tuesday.

"Uncle Max was killed in the house," said Lily.

"Didn't you think of that before?" asked Vaz. "Don't ghosts usually haunt the spots where they died?"

"I don't know what ghosts do! Not real ghosts, anyway." She hadn't known Uncle Max, but he was a member of her family, and it was a horrible way to die. As if there were a good way.

"What's up there?"

"Where?"

"In your attic?"

"I tried to get up there once, but the door was stuck. Oh, god," she said. "When I was looking through the keyhole I thought I smelled smoke."

"We'll break into the attic next," said Vaz. He snapped a picture of the article and tried to close the book. "Come on, Lily, put the book back. We have to go now."

"Wait," she said. She flipped through the rest of the pages.

"Hurry, Lily. He'll be here any minute. We have to go."

"There's more."

Investigators now believe that Maxmillian Wood, killed in a fire in his mother's summer home on Perry Street, may have been responsible for the rash of mysterious fires that have plagued Cape May since 1955. The family vehemently denies these charges. "My son did not set those fires," said Mrs. Joseph Wood. "And we intend to prosecute those who seek to smear my son's name."

Vaz pulled the book out of her hands and hauled her to her feet.

"What are you doing? I want to keep—"

"He's back," he whispered in her ear as he dragged her from the room. "Burton's back."

Chapter 14

L ily could hear the key turning in the front-door lock as they slid down the hallway, sneakers squealing, through the dining room, back toward the door to the basement. Burton swore, muttering to himself in the front entranceway as Lily eased the door closed behind her, wincing as the latch made a little tinny click. She thought she could actually *see* her heart beating through her sweatshirt.

They sneaked down the stairs, stepping lightly so as not to make the rickety old things creak and moan. At the bottom of the short staircase, they stopped to listen. Footsteps thudded directly above, ceased, then thudded again, seeming to move farther away. Lily could feel Vaz's lips against her ear when he whispered, "If he goes in the library, he'll see the books on the floor."

Lily nodded, and they crept toward the open basement window. They stared at it. It hadn't seemed so high coming through the other way. Lily moved some squishy newspapers out of the way, picked up some books, and started stacking them under the window as quickly and quietly as she could. Vaz did the same. There was a hoarse shout from above, and the sound of feet pounding through the house. Lily jumped on top of the books, grabbed the windowsill, wriggling frantically as Vaz pushed at her feet. Vaz jumped up on the books and pulled himself out in one smooth motion. As his sneakers cleared the open window, they heard the basement door open with a bang, and Burton's voice yelling, "Who's there? I know someone's there! I've got a gun, and I'm not afraid to use it!"

Vaz and Lily burst from the bushes and ran through the yard to the red cedar fence that separated Burton's property from Lily's uncle's. They dropped to their knees and crawled behind a thick row of evergreen hedges that grew alongside the fence, scratching their hands and their faces in the process. They both heard the basement window creak in protest as Bailey Burton slammed it shut.

"The fence doesn't go all the way around," whispered Lily. "It stops at the back. We just have to get to the end, and we can sneak into Uncle Wes's yard." They got on their bellies and wormed their way toward the back of the property until they reached the end of the cedar fence, just making it into Uncle Wes's yard when they heard something thrashing the bushes on Burton's side. The air fled Lily's lungs when a knowing voice wafted through the cedar planks.

"I know you're out here," Bailey Burton whispered. "Sneaking through the bushes like dirty little animals."

Lily and Vaz didn't dare move. They waited until the thrashing and the threats subsided—a long time—and they heard Burton walking back toward his house. And then they waited a while longer, just to be sure, until their hands were so cold and stiff that they could barely unclench their fists.

"That was close," whispered Vaz.

"I know."

"He had some nerve calling us dirty."

"I know," said Lily.

"You know what else?"

"What?"

"It's really freaking cold out here."

"You're the idea man," said Lily. "Do you think it's safe to stand up and walk to the back door?"

So they waited even longer, until the sky looked angry and dark and burned around the edges. "Okay," said Lily. "Can you stand up?"

"I think so."

They stood and staggered to the back door, propping themselves up against the house as Lily tried to maneuver the key into the lock, tried to turn it with her rigid hands. She almost cried in relief when the back door finally swung open and they fell into the kitchen. She closed and locked the door behind them and dropped into one of the kitchen chairs.

"Do you think he actually would have shot us?" she said after they had been sitting for a while and she could feel the muscles in her face begin to thaw.

"We don't even know if he had a gun," said Vaz. "I didn't even see him, did you?"

"No. Do you think he knows it was us?"

Vaz squirmed uncomfortably. "Yeah. Who else would it be?"

"A burglar?"

"A burglar that didn't steal anything?" Vaz unzipped his coat. "We were just at his house asking to see some old documents and he tells us get lost, no deal, right?

Then he comes home one day and finds the same documents we asked about all over the floor. What do you think he's going to think?"

"Do you think he'll call the police or something?"

"I don't know."

Lily tugged on her lip with her teeth. "I'm sorry I got you into this."

He shrugged and pulled his camera out of his pocket. "I got myself into this."

Lily asked the question she had been dying to ask. "Why did you get yourself into this?"

"Maybe I like an adventure."

"An adventure?"

"Maybe you do this kind of stuff every other week, but I don't. I've lived in the same place my whole life. Cape May has flower shows, not nightclubs. The biggest thing that ever happened to me is the worst thing that ever happened to me." He looked out the window. "I usually *read* about this kind of stuff—I don't get to live it."

"Oh," she said, amazed that he could think her life was like this all the time.

He reached out and pulled a twig from her hair. "And anyway, maybe I like you. You're pretty funny when you want to be."

Lily stared stupidly at the twig in his hand and tried to think of something cool and funny to say, something that would make him touch her hair again. Then she had to bite her lip harder to keep from laughing at herself. She had just broken into some guy's house; discovered that her uncle's house was haunted by a boy arsonist who had burned to death in the attic; been chased by giant larva with a gun; and here she was, thinking about *guys*.

Vaz was watching her, and she dropped her eyes to her hands. They were dirty and raw and scratched, so she got up to wash them in the sink. "Since we're officially criminals," she said, "why don't we break into the attic? See if anything's there." She scrubbed at her skin, even though the soap stung. "Unless you don't want to."

"I wouldn't want you to call me a girly man or anything."

She couldn't help but smile. "That would be a compliment."

They took off their jackets and Vaz washed his hands, and then they searched the kitchen for things they could use to pick the attic lock—a couple of forks, a plastic toothpick, and an expired phone card that Lily's mother had left on the counter.

As they climbed the main staircase, the phone rang. They looked at each other.

"Bailey?" said Vaz.

"Could be one of those cranks who never says anything," Lily said.

"Won't know unless you answer it."

Lily walked back down the stairs and picked up the receiver with both hands. "Hello?"

"Lily?" The voice sounded as if it hadn't been used in a century.

Lily's stomach lurched. "This is Lily."

"Yes. Well. This is your uncle. Wesley. Your uncle Wesley. Wesley Wood."

"Oh," Lily said. Vaz mouthed *Who is it?*, but Lily waved him off. "How are you?"

Cough. "Fine, thank you. And you?"

"Fine." Lily waited.

"And your mother? How is she?"

Lily switched from one foot to the other. "Fine."

"The two of you are getting along? You're comfortable?"

"Yes, thank you."

"No problems that I need to be aware of?"

"Um . . . no."

"Well, then. Very good to hear."

Silence.

"Are you finding everything you need?"

"Yeah," said Lily. "I think so."

"Are you sure? The house is quite large, though I expect someone your age would have explored every inch of it by now."

"Uh-huh," she said.

Another silence. Lily thought she could hear the grinding of teeth.

"Have I interrupted something?"

"I have a friend over. We're doing homework."

"I won't keep you then. Would you please tell your mother I called?"

"Yeah, okay."

"Very good. Good-bye, then."

"Bye."

Lily hung up the phone and walked back up the stairs. "That was my uncle Wesley."

"Really? What did he say? Why didn't you ask him

anything about the house?"

"He didn't say anything, really. And I didn't want to just babble about ghosts and things. I don't want him to think I'm a total freak."

They reached the stairs to the attic. Vaz pointed to the faint coating of dust on the floor, now stamped with footprints. "Who's been up here before?"

"Me," said Lily.

"Oh. And whose prints are those?"

She saw a smudged set of prints going up the middle of the stairs and coming back down again. But then there was another, clearer set of prints on the left side of the staircase, close to the wall. This set went up, but didn't come back down.

"I think the ghost . . . guy . . . whoever is still up there," said Vaz.

"Unless they came back down the middle, like I did," said Lily.

Vaz pressed his lips together, but Lily knew what he was thinking. What *she* was thinking. That crazy Uncle Max was in the attic. Waiting for them.

Lily grabbed the phone card from Vaz's hand. "Might as well get this over with." She marched up the stairs, deliberately stepping on the prints on the left side. She put her hand on the porcelain knob, expecting it to stick, but almost fell back into Vaz when the knob turned easily in her palm.

She glanced at Vaz, then pushed the door open.

They stepped into the dark.

Lily shook her head. "I don't see anything, do you?"

That's when the door closed softly behind them.

The Phantom
of the Opera

O h, no. No way. Uh-uh. This was NOT happening.
Lola had Steffie's whole makeover planned, and
boy, was it going to be mondo cool: great smeary
pink lips, big orange spots of rouge, blue eye shadow, fake
lashes out to there, hairy beauty mark, the works. But she had
only been able to do the lipstick before Mr. Scary Soot-for-
Breath stormed in and just *shoved* her out of the way! What *was*
that guy's problem? Why would a bit of lipstick get his knickers
in a bunch? Why couldn't he just get a life already?

Er . . . so to speak.

Had Steffie dumped him or something? Had she set his arms
on fire? And what kind of loco death dance was that anyway?
Did he think it was scary? Ha! No way! Lola gnawed at a fingernail. Nope, not scary at all. It was all so desperate and creepy
and overdone, so *Phantom of the Opera*, it just made her sick to
watch.

And now this. The studmuffin had been over a bunch of times
now, but he and Steffie had never gotten, you know, cozy or
anything—he obviously felt sorry for the poor little geek. But
today they decide to go upstairs. Alone. Together. And that
flamey creep just stands by and watches it happen! And then he
closes the door on them!

Lola stomped up the attic stairs after them. She didn't know what kinds of plans Fireball had for Steffie, or what Steffie had done to him in another lifetime, but all Lola knew was that he just better butt out or he could end up decked out in a pink prom gown. Forever. She just wanted to teach Steffie a lesson, that's all, and he would just have to wait his turn.

He didn't *own* the afterlife.

Chapter 15

The door couldn't make up its mind. It opened, then closed, then opened, then slammed shut. They could hear a sharp click as the tumblers in the lock turned.

"Omigod," Lily whispered, barely able to speak. Like in those dreams where you open your mouth and nothing comes out, she had no breath.

"Don't panic," said Vaz. "I think there's a light." He pulled a cord, and a single lightbulb cast a feeble yellow pall over the large room.

Empty.

"There's nothing up here!" said Vaz. Lily thought he sounded disappointed.

"Nope," she agreed. And there wasn't. Not a single stick of furniture, not a box or a book. And certainly no enraged spirits ready to jump them or set them on fire.

"He could still be here," said Vaz.

"Who?" asked Lily, though she knew who. Her heart was still hammering in her chest.

"Remember the breathing in the kitchen? We didn't think there was anyone in the room then, either."

They stood in the center of the room, backs to each other. Lily wasn't sure if she should be scared or angry or confused or what. She was beyond feeling much of anything.

"I don't hear any breathing," Vaz said.

"Me neither."

Vaz cleared his throat. "So if there's nobody here, who closed the door?"

"The wind?"

"What wind?"

"Maybe the door has those hinges on it that makes it slam shut," Lily said, knowing it was dumb as she said it.

"And open and shut and open and shut?" said Vaz. The two of them waited, absorbing the words.

"Maybe we should try the door," Lily suggested. She jiggled the knob. It stuck fast, the way it had when she had first tried to open it all those weeks ago.

"We're locked in," she said.

"Guess so," Vaz said. He walked over and pressed his ear to the door. Then he dropped to his knees and tried to look under the crack at the bottom.

"See anything?" said Lily.

"No."

"Hear anything?"

"No." Vaz got to his feet.

"Do you still think we're having an adventure?"

"Sure, don't you?" He grinned. "You didn't happen to bring any pizza with you, did you?"

"No."

"Cake? Cookies? Popsicles?"

"Sorry."

He went to the window and looked out. "Well, there's

one less evildoer to worry about. Bailey's out wandering around in his backyard. And he doesn't have a gun, you'll be happy to know. He has a badminton racket."

"A badminton racket. Well, maybe it has a death-ray attachment."

"Right," said Vaz. "You know, I bet he was the one who made that phone call a few weeks ago. I bet he was the one who called me Odysseus. What do you think he wants? And what was all that stuff about Ms. Reedy? 'She sent you?'"

Lily shrugged. "I have no idea. War of the librarians?" She sat down and leaned up against the wall, and rubbed her legs with her hands. "She was acting kind of weird, though, don't you think?"

"Ms. Reedy's always weird," said Vaz.

"Yeah, but she kept hovering around us, you know, like she wanted to see what we were doing."

"Either that, or she was afraid we'd blow up the microfilm reader."

"True," said Lily. "Well, you might think this is an adventure, but I'm kind of sick of it all."

"Yeah," said Vaz. He looked at his watch. "My mom's going to kill me if I don't show up sometime this week."

"My mom should be home soon," Lily said. "She'll let us out."

Vaz sat down next to Lily. Lily picked at her fingernails nervously, and Vaz played with the drawstring on the hood of his sweatshirt.

"At least we found out who the ghost is," said Vaz.

"But we still don't know what he wants."

"He probably wants what every ghost wants," Vaz replied.

"What's that?"

"Peace. Isn't that why ghosts haunt people?"

"I don't know why ghosts haunt people," said Lily.

Vaz pulled both ends of the drawstring until they were exactly the same length. "I have to say I was expecting a show when we got up here. At least a bonfire or a mysterious message written in blood on the wall. Something."

"Maybe he's not here," said Lily.

"This is where he died," Vaz said. "Violently, remember?"

Lily thought about that. "Maybe ghosts don't always stay where they die. Maybe they wander around. Maybe they go to the movies."

"The movies?"

"Well, how do we know what ghosts do? Did you ever ask your father?"

Vaz frowned. "I told you, it's not like that. He can't hear me. He doesn't give me advice or anything. We don't chat about politics or the movies. He's *dead*, Lily."

"I'm sorry. I didn't mean to make you mad," Lily said. She chewed on her lip. "I think . . . forget it."

He straightened his legs. "What?"

"I think I'm jealous of you."

"What do you mean?"

"It's going to sound horrible."

"Tell me anyway."

Lily took a deep breath. "I'm jealous that your father still talks to you. I mean, I know he's dead, and I'm sorry for you, but at least he still tries to contact you. My dad left us when I was five and never came back. He's alive, but he might as well be dead." When Vaz was silent, Lily said, "See? I knew it was a horrible thing to say."

"No, I think I know what you mean."

"You do?"

"Yeah. Don't worry about it."

She swallowed hard. She couldn't remember the last time she had said something so terrible but so true. It hurt, but it felt good, too. The way it does when you pull a sliver of glass from your skin.

Her backside started to fall asleep, so she shifted, glanced down at the floor. From the opposite wall toward the middle of the room, the floorboards had a fresh, untouched look, only getting darker and more warped underneath her. She knew then that the opposite side of the floor had been destroyed and replaced, while some of the original flooring had been preserved on the side where she sat. Instinctively she ran her hands along the floor. Her fingernail caught on a groove in the wood.

"Look," she said. "There *is* something up here after all!"

The two of them crouched. A faint heart was scratched into the surface of the wood right beneath the window.

"I can't make it out," said Vaz.

"M," said Lily, running her fingers over the lettering. "M.W. plus A.B. Max. But who is A.B.?"

"I don't know," said Vaz.

"Max loved her," said Lily. Max couldn't be that bad if he loved someone, could he?

She traced the heart with her fingertip a few times before she realized Vaz was staring at her. She glanced up at him, the blood flooding her face. He was so good looking he was almost pretty. If it weren't for the big, bumpy nose, he would be.

He leaned forward, and her stomach flipped over when she realized he was about to kiss her. And then he did, his lips soft and plush as the skin of a peach.

He pulled back, staring again. "Even with the pink clothes and the twigs in your hair, you're so pretty."

She couldn't help it; she touched her fingers to her mouth. "I was thinking the same thing about you."

He looked confused. "That's a weird thing to say to a guy."

"But I mean it."

"Sure. Whatever. Shut up."

"But—"

"Hey, it's been a long day." He leaned forward and kissed her again. Lily felt the blood beating in her ears, felt something inside her, achy and new, open up like a bud.

Then the door flew open and her mother, magnificent in purple and orange, towered over them. "Just what in the name of Pete is going on up here?"

Chapter 16

For three days Lily had to endure her mother's abrupt transformation from fun-loving free spirit to judgmental, overprotective parent: the reproachful glares, tight white lips, endless head shaking, and what-kind-of-child-have-I-raised glances up at the sky.

"What in the world were you thinking, Lily? What happened to that responsible person I left in charge of the house? Do you really think it was okay to spend your days making out with your boyfriend? Did you think I wouldn't find out? I was thirteen once, too, you know."

Lily's face burned, but she did not look up from *Oliver Twist*. Now Lily was forced to go to the Something Fishy gift shop every day to do her schoolwork under her mother's baleful eye. Her mother would not allow her to stay in the house by herself, would not allow Vaz to come over unless they were "supervised." Lily couldn't remember the last time her mother had supervised her, and considering how odd and unconventional her mother's behavior normally was, Lily didn't see why her mother should start doing it now.

Her mother sat at the glass counter, removing pairs of earrings from plastic packets, arranging the pairs on blue velvet display pads. "I feel guilty about uprooting you again. But that doesn't mean you can do anything you want."

Lily turned the page in her book, the letters meaningless squiggles. She was so angry and embarrassed that she had read the same ten pages three times and could barely remember what had happened in them. "I don't think I can do anything I want," she said. "That wasn't what I was doing."

"I don't want to think about what you were doing."

She could still feel Vaz's kisses on her lips, and it made everything go all fuzzy and bright, as if she had looked at the sun too long. "Mom, just a week ago you were talking about what a hot taco Vaz was, and now you're upset? I don't get it."

"A few weeks ago I thought I could trust you to behave responsibly. Now I'm not so sure. Where's my mature, grown-up daughter?"

"I'm right here."

"You don't even know that kid."

"I do, too."

Lily's mother poked a gold earring through the velvet. "What do you know? You don't know anything."

Lily thought of the Computer Geek. Her own father. "You should talk," Lily muttered.

Her mother stopped poking. "What? What did you say?"

"Nothing."

"I am an adult, Lily. You can't compare your life to mine."

"I'm not."

"Yes, you are." Lily's mother finished the earring display

and opened the door of the glass cabinet. "You're mature in a lot of ways, but you're not all grown up yet, no matter what you've been through. What we've been through." She put the velvet card in the case and slid the door shut. "I talked to the school. You start next week. As soon as the store opens."

"But Mom!"

"I'm sorry. I thought I could handle the homeschooling. I thought *you* could handle it, but we obviously can't. So we're going to be normal people and do the normal thing and send you off to school." Her mother gathered up the pile of tiny plastic bags.

Lily shut her book and dropped it to the floor. There was no point in reading it now. "I found out about Uncle Max."

"Found out what?"

"How he died. That's what me and Vaz were doing. Reading old newspapers. Researching his death."

"Researching each other is more like it." Lily's mother threw the bags in the garbage can.

"Why didn't you tell me?"

"Max died years ago. Before I was born. What does that have to do with anything?"

"He's still there, Mom. The noises, the phone calls, the doll in my bed. I found *jam* in my shoes. There's something weird going on. I think maybe the house is—"

Her mother put up a palm. "Stop. Stop it right now."

"Mom, would you just listen?"

"No, I've had it." Her mother's eyes shone with tears. "You don't seem to get it. We have to live in that house.

Making up a bunch of scary stories about it isn't going to help anything. We don't have anywhere else to go, do you understand me?"

"Yes, but—"

"*We have nowhere else to go.*" For a moment her expression softened. "Forget about it, Lily. Please? I'm stuck. You're stuck. This is what we've got. This is all we've got." She straightened, wiped her eyes. "So if my dead, delinquent uncle Max is playing with dolls and making phone calls to China, there's not a heck of a lot we can do about it." She turned and stalked from the room, patchwork skirt streaming out behind her.

Lily sat in her chair, still and stunned. She had only kissed a guy, big deal! What was her mother so angry about? *She* was the one who should be angry! Her mother knew how much it hurt her to make a friend or two only to have to leave them. And no matter how many times her mother said that they were stuck, that this was it, Lily knew they'd leave. They always did.

She got up and stood in front of the big window. The sky was gray and flat as paper, the row of storefronts looking like cutouts against it. Her mother didn't believe that the house was haunted, and Lily still didn't know why Uncle Max was haunting it. What if Uncle Max wanted to do more than just scare them?

Across the street, in the window of the Good Fortunes Shoppe, a fuzzy head appeared. The dandelion woman. The woman who had spied on her mother. Something darted across Lily's brain, a memory, what was it? Something that the woman had said to her mother—something odd.

Suddenly it burned neon across her vision. The woman had run out of her store yelling something about a boy on fire.

A boy on fire.

Max.

Lily read the list on the door of the shop, zooming in on MEDIUM SERVICES AVAILABLE BY APPOINTMENT. Her mother had said mediums talk to ghosts. The woman had seen Uncle Max! And if she could see Uncle Max, she could probably talk to him. But that, Lily thought, was sure to cost money, a lot of money. Where would she get a lot of money?

Lily looked around the gift shop. Maybe she could swipe one of her mother's unset jewels when she wasn't looking—an amethyst or even a ruby. But if her mother caught her . . . well, Lily didn't want to think about that. Besides, she'd feel awful stealing from her mother, no matter how strange and unfair and stupid she was acting.

She tugged at her collar, and her finger slid over the chain around her neck. Would it be enough? Yes, she was sure it would be. She reached around her neck and unclasped the chain, knowing she had no other choice. Lily squeezed the necklace in her palm, then slipped it into the pocket of her jeans.

"Mom?"

"What?"

"I'm hungry. Why don't I go across the street and pick us up some sandwiches for lunch?"

A pause. "You don't have any plans to meet anyone, do you?"

"Mom, it's a school day. Even if I wanted to meet someone, I couldn't." Lily walked to the back of the store and peeked her head into the stockroom, where her mother scribbled something in a logbook. "Come on, Mom. I'll just be a little while. I'm starving."

Her mother opened up her drawstring bag and pulled out a rumpled ten-dollar bill. "Just sandwiches, okay? We can drink water from the cooler. And no wandering off."

"Okay." Lily reached out for the money, but her mother grabbed her hand instead.

"I want the best for you. I want you to be happy. You know that, don't you?"

The pendant dug into Lily's hipbone. "I know."

Madame Durriken's fortune

madame Durriken had tried reading the tarot, the I-Ching, the crystal ball. She had attempted to put herself into a trance and send her spirit into another astral plane. She had even called on that silly twit over on Jackson, Fortuna de Luck, but the fraud simply piped in some "ghostly" voices over the intercom and tried to charge fifty dollars for the privilege of listening to them. What was the world coming to?

She bit into a slice of cold pizza that she'd had to pry from the box with a letter opener shaped like a dragon's head. Not a single customer had darkened her door in days; even papery old Mrs. Wilma Hines—she of the wayward checkbook—stayed home. Just as well, thought Madame Durriken. The shoppe was a disaster. Fortune-telling paraphernalia littered the tables and counters, satin capes and cloaks puddled on the floor because Madame Durriken—frustrated with another failed attempt at contacting the ghost—had ripped them from their hangers and stomped on them.

Some time off, yes, that's what she needed. A little vacation, somewhere nice and warm. The Bahamas? Somewhere in Mexico? Or Egypt. Now that would be wonderful. She had heard that Egyptian men favored pale women. Or was it plump women? She pried another slice of pizza from the box.

A knock on the door startled her, and she dropped the pizza into her lap. "Crap and crappola," she muttered, then stood and wiped at the sauce on her yellow caftan. The knocking became more insistent, and Madame Durriken was stricken with the idea that it was the ghost boy hammering his flaming fists on the door. What to do, what to do?

She grabbed the dragon letter opener and gripped it in her fist like a dagger before moving slowly to the door. With a bony finger, she pulled the curtain away from the window, looked out, and sighed with relief. Just a kid. Madame Durriken scanned the brick walk for the ghost, but he had disappeared. She hid the letter opener behind her back and threw open the door.

"What?" she barked.

The girl shivered in her thin coat. "I want . . . I need a reading done."

Madame Durriken eyed the girl's clothes suspiciously. "Do you have money? This isn't a charity, you know."

The girl glared, reached into her pocket, and pulled something out. "I have this." She dangled a silver pendant on a chain in front of Madame Durriken's eyes.

Madame Durriken took the necklace, hefted it in her hand. The chain was smooth and light as a trickle of water, but the pendant itself was more interesting. Symbols carved in its battered surface hinted at something ancient, something mystical and magical and . . . expensive. She could get a hundred fifty dollars for it, easy. She smiled. "Come in, dear."

The girl stepped into the store, unzipping her jacket. Her eyes widened as she looked around. "What happened? Were you robbed or something?"

"Just doing a little inventory, that's all. I'm sorry about the mess. I don't normally do much business this time of year." The girl was tall for her age, with extremely long, untidy reddish hair, ragged little eyebrows, and pale skin. A pretty young thing, but fierce. Her green eyes were hungry, draped underneath with dark circles. Madame Durriken smiled. She loved the hungry ones; they always came back for more.

But she seemed familiar. "Haven't we met somewhere before, dear?"

"Probably. My mother works across the street. At the gift store? I've been there a couple of times. I've seen you looking out your window."

Madame held her breath. "Your mother is blond? With an orange cloak?"

"That's her."

"I see," said Madame Durriken, mind racing. The ghost boy often followed the blond woman to the store. What was this? A trick? She led the girl to the table at the front of the store, surreptitiously biting down on the silver pendant. It was genuine, she was sure of it. She clasped the necklace at the back of her neck and arranged it on the yellow caftan.

"What's your name, my dear?"

"Lily."

"Sit down, Lily, and explain what you need me to do."

"I want you to contact a dead person."

Madame Durriken's brows were swallowed by her fluffy hair. "Someone specific?"

"My uncle Max."

"And why would you like to contact your uncle Max?"

"Because he's haunting us, that's why." Her green eyes dared

Madame Durriken to disagree. "I want to know what he wants."

So do I, you little ragamuffin, thought Madame Durriken. *And when I can be sure that he's YOUR business, I can get back to my business. For example, how many more necklaces you will bring me.* "Of course . . . er, Lily, is it? Lily. Has your uncle ever appeared to you? Have you seen him?"

"I kind of thought you had," said the girl.

"Whatever do you mean?" said Madame Durriken.

The girl smiled a knowing smile that Madame Durriken didn't care much for. "My mom told me how you ran out of your store yelling about a boy who was on fire."

"Dear, I never *yell.* Perhaps your mother was mistaken. So I take it that you've never seen your uncle yourself?"

"There was a painting on the wall."

"What does he look like?" said Madame Durriken, trying to keep the eagerness out of her voice.

"Light hair, grayish kind of skin. Weird green eyes." The girl tipped her head, considering. "I think he looked like a ghost even before he was a ghost."

That's him, thought Madame, *that's the crazy bugger.* "Uh-huh. What's been happening to make you believe that your uncle is haunting you?"

"The phone rings and there's nobody on the other end. My books and some other things have been moved to different places. I've heard footsteps and weird breathing when no one was there. Other stuff."

"But you've never seen him in his ghostly form?"

"No," said Lily.

"Are you sure?"

"Yes, I'm sure," said Lily, crossing her arms.

"Of course you are," soothed Madame Durriken. "Why don't you tell me everything you know about him."

"I don't know much. He died before I was born. In a fire in the attic. The newspapers said that he set it himself as a prank, but then he got trapped."

Stupid, thought Madame Durriken. When she was a child, her brother had accidentally set the family trailer on fire, killing Madame's ant farm. She'd hated the trailer, but she had never forgiven her brother for killing the ants.

"Do you know how old your uncle was, Lily?"

"Seventeen, I think. A few years older than me."

"Was anyone else harmed in the fire?"

"I don't think so."

"Do you know where he's buried?"

"No. But I know he had a funeral. It said so in the paper."

Madame Durriken sat back in her chair, hoping the relief wasn't visible on her face. Nothing for her to worry about, no connection to her at all! Thank goodness! She'd seen enough movies in which people were haunted until they solved a crime or found the bones and gave them a proper burial or some other such nonsense, and Madame was not looking forward to *that*. A stupid kid gets himself killed, then spends the rest of eternity doing a jig in the Cape May mall, driving his relatives nuts. It was hilarious when you thought about it.

As soon as the silly twit left, Madame decided, she would call that guy who did the Cape May ghost tours and let him know all about the fire boy on the mall. With the mall added to the tour, Madame Durriken was sure to make a mint from all the amateur spirit seekers.

Madame's thoughts cheered her, and she began to shuffle the

tarot cards. Now that the mystery of the ghost boy was solved, she intended to have a little fun.

"What are those?" Lily asked.

"These are tarot cards, dear. They help a psychic divine the future." Madame spoke slowly, as if talking to the slow or foreign.

"Will they help you talk to Uncle Max?"

"In a minute. It's important to establish the energies that surround you."

Madame Durriken bestowed her wisest, most trustworthy smile on the girl and pushed the deck at her. "Please shuffle the deck seven times. When you are finished, cut the deck into three piles."

The little urchin did as she was told, and Madame Durriken commenced the "reading." As usual, she kept very still and silent as she gazed at the cards, a little concerned frown playing at her brows. (She had perfected this look in the mirror.) She waited until her client was nearly shaking with suspense before murmuring, "There's a young man."

"Max?"

"No, a living young man. Do you know of whom I speak?"

The girl bit her lip, then nodded.

"Are you . . . involved with this young man?"

Another cautious nod.

Madame Durriken paused for effect. "Perhaps you did not take the time to get to know this young man as well as you should have."

The girl started, blinking heavily. Madame almost brayed with the deliciousness of the moment. The young ones were so easy to play that she almost felt guilty. Almost.

"I understand how that can happen, believe me. I was young

162

once. But I must warn you that this boy is up to no good."

The girl found her voice. "I don't know what you mean."

"See the cards, here and here?" She flicked a hand at random cards in the spread. "It seems that you are not the only young lady that this boy is . . . um . . . oh, dear, how shall I put it? You're not the only young lady he's *associating* with."

"I don't know what you're talking about."

"I'm sorry to be the bearer of bad news," said Madame Durriken. "He's got other girlfriends." She pointed to a card on which was a picture of a fair-haired girl with two cups. "There's a blonde. And probably more. A couple of blondes. You're being played for a fool, child," said Madame Durriken. She held up the remains of a slice of pizza. "Do you mind if I eat while we talk?"

"What? Uh, no." The girl looked as if she had been slapped. She rubbed her lips with her fingertips.

"Cheer up, dear. There are many other fish in the sea, as I'm sure your mother would tell you."

The girl frowned. "What are you saying about my mother?"

A touchy one, that was for sure. What fun. "Nothing, dear, nothing at all. I'm just trying to tell you that there will be plenty of other young men." Madame Durriken knew that the silly girls never wanted to hear about the other young men coming along, that it just made them feel worse. "But I do see that you do very well in school," said Madame Durriken, chewing loudly. "And I see that you will become very popular, very, very popular, sometime soon. This spring, I think. I suggest cheerleading. The universe says that you would make a wonderful cheerleader."

The girl gripped the armrests of her chair, gaping at her in horror. Madame smiled blandly back, taking another bite of pizza to hide her amusement. As she watched, the girl turned her head away and swallowed hard several times. Then she said, "Can we please talk to my uncle now?"

"Wouldn't you like to know the name of your future husband? I'm seeing the letter H. Huey? Huckleberry?" She closed her eyes and put an index finger to her temple. "Give me a minute, it will come to me—"

"Did you hear that?" said the girl.

Madame's eyes flew open. "Hear what?"

"I don't know. I thought I heard someone whispering."

Madame heard it then, barely, a dry scratchy sound that made her knees turn to water. She looked down, a moan strangling in her throat.

The tarot cards were assembling themselves into a pile, as if invisible hands scraped them together. The cards dragged against the tablecloth, making a chafing sound. Neither Madame Durriken nor Lily moved a muscle, mouths slack with shock.

A card flipped over on its back, landing face up in front of Madame Durriken. Madame stared. "M—Max?" she said. "Is that you?"

The card flipped over again, facedown, then flipped face up again.

"Read it," the girl said.

Madame Durriken looked down at the card. There was a picture of a ship with several torches burning on deck. "Er . . . smooth sailing?"

A lightbulb in the fixture over the door burst, raining slivers of frosted glass on the carpeting.

The girl watched the glass settle on the floor. "Try again."

"Happy trails?"

The front door opened, letting in a blast of freezing air, then slammed shut.

"Um, a vacation? Traveling for business?"

The dragon-shaped letter opener whipped through the air and stuck in the wall over Madame Durriken's head.

"Are you reading the card?" said the girl.

"Yes, I'm reading the card!" hissed Madame Durriken.

"He's trying to tell us something. What's the card supposed to mean?"

"How should I know?" Madame Durriken shrieked. "It's a picture of a stupid ship!" She looked up at the ceiling. "It's just a boat!"

The card flew off the table, and another took its place.

"You mean it *was* a boat?" said Madame Durriken.

The new card depicted a man with a crown of leaves sitting on a throne, another man begging at his feet.

"A king," barked Madame Durriken.

A figurine of Merlin suddenly rolled off its pedestal on the counter and landed with a dull thud on the carpeting. It continued to roll until it hit the wall. Then it backed up, hit the wall. Backed up, hit the wall.

"That's not it," said the girl, her eyes as wide as dinner plates. "You're a big help."

Merlin crashed into the wall, *thud, thud, thud*.

"A prince," said Madame Durriken.

"A man," said the girl. "A father. Wait! A brother."

The card flew off the table. A new card replaced it. This showed a beautiful, black-haired woman walking naked from the sea.

"A woman," said Madame Durriken.

165

The coat tree fell over, smashing a glass display case.

"The ocean," said Madame Durriken.

One by one the crystal balls on the shelf exploded, as if they were no more substantial than balloons. "*Playboy!*" shouted Madame Durriken, a cold sweat breaking on her forehead. "MTV!"

"The beach?" the girl said. Again the card flew from the tabletop to the floor, and was quickly replaced.

The next card depicted a dancing clown skipping down an open road. The Fool. Madame put her face in her hands. For the first and the last time in her life, she knew exactly what that tarot card meant, exactly what she would have to do.

She did not say a word, but she didn't have to. The cards suddenly took wing and flapped to the floor like broken birds. Merlin made one last run at the wall, then rolled onto his back, still. The clasp on the necklace shuddered and opened, and the pendant fell from Madame Durriken's neck and landed on the table. Like some metallic tadpole, the necklace snaked toward the girl, and then stopped.

The girl looked down at the necklace, then up at Madame Durriken. She was trembling like a hungry kitten. "I . . . I think he wants me to have it."

"Take it," said Madame Durriken. "Take anything. How about a piece of pizza?"

Madame leaped to her feet and grabbed an armful of the moon-embroidered cloaks and a large carpet bag. She reached into one of the smashed display cases and grabbed handfuls of jewelry. She threw the jewelry into the bag and watched as the girl scooped up the silver necklace with shaking fingers, closed the clasp, and shoved the necklace into her pocket. Madame kicked the coat tree out of the way to open the door for them both.

"If you're ever in South Carolina," Maple Ann Spatz said, "do me a favor? Don't look me up."

Chapter 17

Breathless and reeling, Lily ran from the diner back to Something Fishy.

"Long line?" her mother said as Lily handed her the sandwich.

"Yeah," said Lily.

Her mother opened the wrapping and picked the lettuce off the bread. "Are you all right? You're white as a gho—" She coughed. "Never mind. Eat your sandwich."

The rest of the afternoon Lily's thoughts spun like hot socks in a dryer. If she had doubted that there were ghosts, she didn't anymore. Max had practically wrecked The Good Fortunes Shoppe. But, Lily thought, he hadn't really hurt anything, had he? At least, he hadn't hurt her or Madame What's-Her-Face. Did this mean that he *wasn't* dangerous? Maybe he wanted Lily to do something, something that would put him, as Vaz had suggested, "at peace." A boat, a brother, a beach. Clues, obviously, but what did they mean?

Boat, brother, beach. Like something from one of those bad books you had to read in first grade: *See the MAN on the BOAT!* Maybe Uncle Max had a boat. She remembered something Vaz had said about a boat when they were in Bailey's library. What was it? Yes! One of the mysterious fires that Max set had burned a boat! But why would Max burn up his own boat? What was that stuff about the brother? Was he talking about Wes or himself? And what was she supposed to think about the strawberry jam? How did that fit in?

She rubbed her temples. She had found out so much in the last week, but none of it made any sense. It was like trying to understand a whale by pressing your nose up to it; she was too close to it to see the whole thing. She wanted to talk to Vaz.

But then she thought about what Madame Durriken had said. That Vaz was no good, that he had other girl-friends. *Blond* girlfriends. Like Kami. Dandelion Woman hadn't been able to read a single tarot card in the way that Max wanted her to. But then, Max didn't seem to want her to read them the regular way. Madame was a greedy dried-up old twig, but did that make her a total fake?

Lily slumped at the glass counter, too tired to think anymore. She rested her head in her arms and soon she was asleep, dreaming that she and her mother were sailing a boat—not on the water, but through a storm cloud—toward a pot of gold at the end of a fuzzy, indistinct rainbow.

That night dinner was popcorn, sliced apples, and cheese in the TV room, with both a warm fire and bright TV flickering as distractions. Lily flipped the channels so fast that her mother claimed it was like looking out the window of a moving train. Lily was relieved when her mother got bored and dizzy and finally went off to bed, leaving Lily with her jumbled thoughts and a quietly purring Julep.

Three hours and the phone hadn't rung, not even for a crank call. Lily wondered if Vaz had tried to reach her, but since there was no answering machine, there was no way to know. He liked Kami, Lily could tell, but he could have changed his mind. Didn't people change their minds all the time? And, just this once, couldn't someone change his mind to include Lily rather than cutting her out?

Her stomach felt like a living thing, like a crab scuttling around, pinching her from the inside. Lily thought about what Vaz had said, how he thought she had lived an adventurous life. It hadn't *felt* like an adventure. She remembered all those dinners with all her mother's boyfriends, remembered the expressions on their faces as they watched her mother talk, laughing, joking, waving her pink-tipped hands. Those guys thought that Lily's mother was one big adventure wrapped in an orange cloak. What if Vaz thought Lily was like that and then found out that she wasn't? Would he leave the way all her mother's boyfriends had, the way her father had?

Lily turned off the TV and stared into the flames. She found that if she let her eyes lose focus, the flames looked like tiny writhing people with streaming yellow hair and hearts of blue. She wondered if that was what Uncle Max had seen in fires, if that was why he set them. Why *had* he set them? Was he a terrible person? Was he crazy? Was he jilted by A. B.? She wished she could ask him.

Why not ask him?

Lily sat up as straight as she could in the squishy furniture, her crab stomach jittering wildly. Never in a million years would she have imagined she would be trying
to talk to a ghost. "Max?" she whispered. Louder. "Uncle
Max?"

The fire danced and Julep stretched, but the rest of the
room was still as a church. "I don't know what you're trying to tell me. I don't know what you want me to do."

She closed her eyes and willed herself to relax, hoping
that she would sense Max's presence in her skin, a cold
wind, a chill finger on her arm. "Uncle Max? My mom's
getting mad, and I go back to school in a week. I don't
have much time. Do you need me to find something or
someone? Would it help? Would you find peace then?"

A log in the fire snapped loud as a gunshot, and Lily
opened her eyes and whipped her head around to see not
Max, but the larval head of Bailey Burton glaring in the
window. She blinked and he was gone.

She hugged herself, feeling a pulse all the way down to
her toes. She knew two things at once, as sure as she knew
that snow was cold and the sun hot: that it was Bailey
Burton's hand she had seen pressed in the window the first
week they had arrived, that it was Bailey Burton who had
been watching her that first day on the beach.

The next morning Lily stumbled half asleep into the
kitchen for breakfast. She hadn't slept well, dreaming that
her hair had gotten caught in the propeller of a boat that
then dragged her around the ocean. Her scalp ached.

Her mother's eyes trailed her around the kitchen as Lily got herself juice and made some toast. When she sat down to eat, her mother placed the coffee mug on the table and heaved a long sigh.

"I see now why you wanted to stay up late last night," she said. "Fine. But understand that I've been there and done that. You'll get sick of it in about a week." She got up and stalked from the room.

Lily put her toast back on her plate. What would she get sick of? Vaz? Kissing? How about getting sick of her mother being a cryptic wacko?

Lily, who suddenly didn't feel like eating, threw away her toast and poured the juice down the sink, then stomped upstairs to brush her teeth and take a shower. It was only when she was squeezing paste onto the toothbrush that she looked in the mirror and understood what her mother was talking about.

Her hair was pink.

Not just pink, but bright hot pink from root to tip, as if someone had leached out all the natural color first and dumped the dye on afterward. She lifted a hank and gaped at the nearly fluorescent strands, shiny and artificial as doll's hair. But why? Why would Max do this? What could it mean? Her eyes stung as she realized that it was the only thing about her looks that she had ever been even a little proud of, the reddish hair she'd gotten from her father. And now it was gone.

Her mother paused at the door of the bathroom. "It looks terrible, in case you were wondering. But, hey, if that's what you want . . ."

Lily bit back the tears and scooped up her comb. "Yes, it's what I want," she said, yanking the comb through, wincing, wondering what Vaz would do when he saw it. "I think it looks great."

"Great!" her mother said, her bright tone as artificial as Lily's hair. "But when you don't want it anymore, don't expect me to pay to get it fixed. It will have to grow out."

"Fine," said Lily, furious at her mother, furious at Max, furious at the world. She threw the comb in the sink, where it spun around and around.

That afternoon, so tired of her mother's disapproving looks, so antsy and out of sorts that she had even tried finishing *Oliver Twist*, Lily begged her mother to let her go to the beach.

"I'm uncomfortable with the idea of you going without supervision," her mother said, setting her mouth in a tight seam.

"Mom. It's a public beach. It's twenty degrees outside. My hair is the color of bubble gum. Trust me when I say it will be me and the seagulls. What's going to happen?"

"I don't know. And that's what I'm afraid of."

Lily almost cried in frustration. "Are you going to keep me a prisoner the rest of my life?"

Her mother had the nerve to look hurt. "You're not a prisoner."

"You could have fooled me," said Lily, throwing herself into a chair. "You let me drive a car when I was eleven years old. And now I can't walk two blocks by myself without you freaking out. What's wrong with this picture?"

Her mother plucked at the folds of her skirt. "Do you want to know what I heard on the radio the morning we left Montclair? Just a few hours before Frank, I mean, the Geek, asked us to go?"

More riddles. Sometimes her mother talked like a character out of *Batman*: "So, Batman, do you want to know why I've kidnapped Robin and hung him upside down over a pit of snakes?"

"I have no idea what you heard on the radio," Lily said.

Lily's mother sat, removed her rings one by one, shook them like dice in her fist. "British researchers found out that money really can buy happiness."

"What?"

"I'm not joking. They studied a large group of people for years, especially those people who came into a large inheritance or won the lottery. Wanna know how much happiness costs these days? About one point seven million dollars. Apparently one point seven million would put a smile on the face of the most miserable person on earth." She shook her head sadly. "I couldn't believe it when I heard it. It was like the world was conspiring to prove me wrong."

Lily had always worried that one day her mother would pass from kooky to totally nuts. "Mom, I don't know what you're talking about."

"You know now that my family, *your* family, has suffered a lot of tragedies. The money was the only thing that stayed constant. Unlike people, money won't let you down, money won't die. Money will save you!" She laughed, but it wasn't a happy sound. "So everyone was obsessed with it. My parents, my uncle, all of them. I wanted no part of it. I wanted love, not money. That's why I ran away with your father." She laughed again, a bray, a sob. "And we both know how that turned out. Your father thought *I* was too straitlaced, too rigid. Me!"

Her mother put her rings back on. "I've been doing a lot of thinking. Maybe your father was right and it's in my genes. Maybe my family was on to something. It's a crazy world." She looked around the shop, her expression saying that evidence of the craziness was apparent in the beach-glass lamps and bikini earrings. "I think about all those times you told me that you were worried about money and that maybe I should be, too, and I think you were right." She looked pointedly at Lily's hair.

An alarm bell clanged in Lily's head. "No, I wasn't. I was wrong. Totally wrong. I was just a snotty kid."

"Even with the hair, you're a wonderful kid."

Lily didn't want to be wonderful and didn't want to be right. She had never seen her mother look so lost and uncertain, and it scared her in a way that no ghost could have scared her. No matter what crazy, crackpot scheme her mother cooked up, she had always seemed hopeful, sure the future would be better. Now Lily felt as if the ground were shifting, turning everything upside down. And what was worse, Lily was the one who had set the ground in motion.

"I just want to do the right thing," her mother said. "I hope I'm not too late."

Lily wriggled in her chair, too confused to find the

words for the horrible feeling welling up inside her. She couldn't stand to look at her mother's twisted, cracked-egg face for another second. Nothing about this was normal. Not Arden Crabtree normal.

"In less than a week I'll be back in school and I'll have tons of structure and supervision and homework and everything else," Lily said. "But now I'm going to the beach. I'll see you back at the house."

She didn't wait for an answer. She got up, put on her coat, and walked—practically ran—out, pulling her ski cap low over her head and tucking all her hair into it. She expected her mother would follow, but she didn't.

As Lily marched away from the store, she couldn't help but notice that cold and lifeless Cape May was shaking itself out of its winter coma. A few people now studded the streets and restaurants, and bills and signs announcing a family roller-skating party and murder mystery dinner theater plastered many store windows. Lily wondered if her mother's new, more responsible parental persona included roller skating, or if she would now think roller skating was too dangerous. The thought wasn't even a bit funny.

Lily reached the promenade and hopped down the steps to Congress Beach. She didn't feel like sitting at the beach, but she did anyway, beginning a new sand house, all the while keeping an eye on the boardwalk for Bailey Burton. Scratching and digging and packing the sand until her hands were red claws and the sun began its daily drift to the west, she erased thoughts of her mother's strange speech at the gift shop, her own flaming pink head. She gave the elaborate sand house one last once-over, straightening the stones she had used to line the front walkway, and then stood.

That's when she saw Vaz strolling down the boardwalk. Arm in arm with Kami.

"You won't believe what I saw," said the man, panting as he fell onto the beach blanket. "A kid with his hands on fire. *Both* hands."

"You did watch where you were walking, didn't you?" the woman asked, smoothing the skirt of her polka-dotted bathing suit. "You didn't knock over that little girl's sand castle again?"

"Did you hear what I said? A kid's hands were on fire!"

"Yes, I heard you. And I think you've had too much sun. You may not think sand castles are important, but that girl worked very hard."

The man grunted, wriggling his large body down next to hers. "Why are you always nagging me? For your information, I didn't knock over the kid's castle, all right?"

The woman yanked the skirt of her bathing suit out from under the man's rump. "Then why is she hiding behind that dune like that? Why does she look so upset?"

"How the heck should I know? Maybe she's a crybaby."

The woman shook her head, the rubber flowers on her bathing cap fluttering like many multicolored wings. "You're as cold as ice. Sometimes I wonder if you even have a drop of blood in your veins."

The man frowned, scratching at his blue legs. "Sometimes I

wonder about that, too. Hey, did you see the guy in the feathered hat? I think he's got some sort of sword."

"You're not even listening to me."

The man picked up a shell and pitched it at the water. "Why bother? You always say the same thing."

Chapter 18

"That boy called again."

Lily felt like throwing up. "So?"

Her mother stood in the doorway of Lily's room. "I just wanted to let you know, that's all."

"Thanks," said Lily. She had the silver pendant in her fingers, turned it over and over and over. Her pink hair was wet and her fingers all pruney from the hour and a half she had spent soaking in the bathtub.

Her mother crossed her arms over her chest and leaned against the doorjamb. "I never said that you couldn't talk to the kid ever again."

"I know."

"He can come over when I'm home. You guys can watch TV." She laughed a little. "He'll probably think your hair is cool."

Lily shrugged. The whole thing was so stupid and crazy it was almost funny. "Flower-Child Mom Catches Kid Kissing Boy, Turns into Soccer Mom! Boy Revealed as Two-Timing Teen! Girl Doesn't Date Again Till She's 35! Ghost Feels Neglected, Misunderstood!"

"Did something happen?"

"No," said Lily.

"Anything you want to talk about?"

Lily kept her face neutral. "No."

Her mother hovered in the doorway, wearing her awful watery expression of uncertainty and concern. "Well, if you want to talk about it, I'll be downstairs."

Lily slipped the pendant around her neck. "Sure."

Her mother's footsteps faded and Lily lay back down. She clutched the necklace hard enough to tattoo the image into her palm. She had been stupid again, more stupid than she had ever been. From now on, she would only believe in what she could see, taste, hear, smell, and touch. No, not even that much. She would only believe in what she could *prove*. What she could hold in her hands and know was real. A rock. A cat. An ant. These noises and clues and hints and visions and everything else were nothing. You couldn't take a picture of a ghost. You couldn't slice a kiss and put it on a slide.

She rolled over onto her side. So she would go to school. She was smart; she could do school, she'd done it before, whatever color her hair was. She'd ace math and science, and in English she'd take their dumb essay tests and she'd write exactly what they wanted her to: "In *Oliver Twist*, Nancy is a sympathetic character because . . . " But inside she would know. It's just a little dream, a bit of fluff, a fantasy. These people don't exist. They're like imaginary friends that little kids have so that they don't feel so afraid and alone.

They are ghosts talking to ghosts.

Heart

*L*ola flopped down on the bed next to Steffie's mom, crossing and uncrossing her arms in annoyance.

The Siamese cat gathered itself in a little loaf on the dresser top, its blue eyes shining rebuke through the dark of the room.

"Oh, what are you looking at?" Lola snapped. The Siamese yawned, and Lola looked away.

The cat mewled and Lola gave it a half-hearted raspberry. The whole plan was going down the toilet, she had to admit. Okay, *had gone* down the toilet. And now it was time to face the facts:

Fact One: Steffie was actually wearing all the pink-splotched clothes like she didn't have a dime to replace them. No tears, no satisfying tantrums, just pulled on the pink-splotched socks and the pink-splotched T-shirt and pink jeans and got on with her day as if everyone walked around looking like a strawberry sundae.

Fact Two: The girl had no life. No cheerleading tryouts for Lola to ruin, no play auditions, no tests, no chance for a public humiliation. The geek didn't even belong to the science club!

Fact Three: the hair! Lola'd had to wait until the Walking Zippo left so that she could get to work, quietly working Screamin' Sally's Punk Rock Pink through each strand of Steffie's hair, and what does Steffie do when she sees herself looking like

Dyeing Disaster Barbie? Nothing! No mondo sessions at the salon, no boxes of Clairol all over the bathroom. She stuffs the hair into a hat, puts on a brave face. It was like Steffie knew she deserved to be punished for what she'd done, and she was just trying to be dignified about it.

All this could only mean one thing.

It wasn't Steffie.

She jumped off the bed and went to the closet, pulled out all the shoes, and began to tie them together in a long footwear chain. It was *his* fault. The Human Torch. Firefly. Phantom of the Opera. If he hadn't interfered and made her so mad, maybe she wouldn't have worked so hard to get revenge. A few splotched clothes, a few moans and rattling, some freaky *Sunset Boulevard* makeup, that would have been it. No real harm done. Now this poor, pathetic geeky girl—whoever she was—had pink hair and pink clothes and sticky shoes and no more foxy boyfriend to suck face with, while the real Steffie was free to keep stealing other people's roles whenever and wherever she wanted.

So uncool. Lola threaded the laces between her teeth and pulled to tighten the knots.

The blond woman rolled over in her sleep, mumbling, "Spaghetti would be nice."

Lola agreed. Spaghetti. And cake. Lola ached for cake. A great big frosty cake with pink roses that said CONGRATULATIONS TO OUR BIGGEST STAR in green icing.

But there would be no cake. Yet.

She got up and crept downstairs, trying to be quiet for once. Lola looked up at the chandelier and shook her head. Funky things going on in this place. Way too funky, if you asked her. A new feeling rose up in her, something she'd never experienced before: guilt. The firefly guy was bad news for sure. Maybe she should stay and try to help the little geeky girl (or at least pluck her eyebrows a bit, jeesh).

"Have some guts," she muttered. "Have some heart."

Nah! What was she thinking? That wasn't even Lola's song! The girl would be okay, right? Pink hair was kinda cool, especially if you were one of those new-wavers, and who knew? Maybe she could start a trend. And there were plenty more fish in the sea, guywise.

It was time for Lola to give it up and hit the beach before there was trouble.

"So long, Human Torch!" she sang, unaware that her voice sounded like the moan of a sick dog, the creak of an old door. "So long, pathetic geeky loser girl!

"Think pink!"

The Lily Song

t he Lily song goes like this: "Lilylilylilylilylilylilylily," sung faster and faster until you can't say it one more time. This is Lily's favorite song. This is the song Lily's father is singing.

Lily is just five, clutching her favorite toy, a large plastic fish that she won't go anywhere without. It is three in the morning, and her mother would be upset to know that she is awake, but it is her secret. Hers and her father's.

Every Friday Lily wakes up in the middle of the night to wait for her father to come home from the club where he plays the guitar. She huddles on the couch with Chucklehead—the fish— and waits, the shadows making monsters on the walls. But she waits anyway, and she isn't frightened, okay, she's not *that* frightened, because her father never makes her wait too long before he turns the key in the door and throws it open, his guitar rising like a black moon behind him.

"Time for bed, Chucklehead," says her father, what he always says, after he has played the Lily song five or ten times in a row.

"One more?"

Lily's father reaches out and puts a large warm hand on her head. "You'll be sleepy in the morning. You don't want to snooze in your cereal, do you?"

Lily giggles. "No. But I'm not that tired. Can you tell me a story?"

"It's too late and I don't want your mom to get mad. Besides, don't you get enough stories in school?"

"I don't like school, Daddy. It's boring. The teacher doesn't tell stories good as you."

"She just needs a little more practice, sweetheart. Give her a chance."

Lily thinks about this for a minute. Her new teacher, Ms. Seaply, was young and pretty and very nervous. She cried once when the kids in her class refused to stop making crazy faces during naptime. Lily felt sorry for her and pretended to be asleep to make her feel better.

"Okay, I'll give her a chance. But I don't think it will do any good."

"Probably not." Her father laughs and scoops her up, nuzzling her neck and making her giggle. He carries her to her bed. "Taco time!" he says, and bundles her up in her blankets.

"Chuckle, too," she says, and her father tacos the fish with an afghan.

"You're getting a little old for Mr. Chuckle here, aren't you?" he says.

"That's what Mommy always says," says Lily. "But I'm not."

"There will come a day you won't need him anymore," says her father.

"Yes, but I'll still *like* him," says Lily.

"You could change your mind," says her father. "People change their minds all the time."

"I could, but I won't," says Lily, and yawns.

Lily falls asleep with her father's hand on her cheek. Her father tucks the blankets around her and kisses her good-night. He stands and watches her for a few moments, the way he always does, before going off to bed.

Lily turns over in her sleep, and Chucklehead the fish slips out of her arms, sliding quietly down between the bed and the wall. The next morning, when Lily cries, confused and frantic, her mother will tell her that he was lonely for his fishy friends and had stolen away during the night, swimming through the drain-pipes to his home in the sea.

Chapter 19

Lily felt as if an animal crouched on her chest. She opened her eyes, gasping for breath. "Daddy?" she whispered. She sat up. The red room looked bloody in the gloom. Julep slept soundly, little paws crossed, at the end of the bed.

A dream. That's all. Just another stupid, stupid dream.

Lily curled in a ball and screwed her eyes shut, willing herself not to cry. She did not want to cry again; she was so tired of crying.

But the day and the dream were too much for her, and soon she was muffling exhausted sobs in her pillow. Behind her the door creaked open, and Lily could hear her mother creep into the room. At the sound Julep opened her eyes and lifted her head, yawned, and put her head back down.

"I'm sorry I woke you up," Lily said into her fists. She felt the bed shift beneath her as her mother sat down on the edge of it. "I had a dream, but I'm okay now." Her mother put her hand on Lily's hair, stroking softly, kindly, and Lily felt another rush of tears. As she cried, her mother's hand gently lifted her hair, combing through the strands, the fingertips brushing against her aching scalp. "Mom," Lily said. "Why did he have to leave? Why does everyone leave?"

Her mother had no answer but to place a hand on Lily's neck, cooling Lily's heated skin. Out the window facing the street, the stars glittered bright as diamonds on velvet. Years before, when Lily was small, her father had told her a story about the beginning of time. "God took up handfuls of dust and wind and light and scattered them into the night. Some of the dust caught in the thick black sky. The dust became stars—blue stars, the hottest; yellow, medium-hot; and red, the coolest. The other particles came to rest on the earth, where they burrowed into the ground like seeds. From those seeds, roses and pansies and parsley and chuckleheads and the most beautiful lilies grew. But those lilies are like stars, see? They're sisters, made of the same funky stuff." He showed her how she could reach up her hand and it would seem as if she were able to hold them in her palm anytime that she wanted to. That they were always with her, and she would never be alone.

"I know," Lily said, "you said we shouldn't blame ourselves. But sometimes I do. And please don't be mad, please. . . ," she said, her voice cracking. "Sometimes I even blame you." But her mother did not stop her gentle, soothing strokes. "If I just knew why, maybe it would be easier. Don't you think it would be easier? Don't you? Mom?"

Lily rolled over to face her mother, only to find the bed empty, except for the Kewpie propped on the pillow beside her.

Chapter 20

Friday, her last day of freedom. Her mother hadn't argued when, after breakfast, Lily refused to go to Something Fishy, when she said that she wanted to stay home and get her clothes ready for school, maybe go to the library to return some books.

"Well, all right," said her mother, wringing her hands. "You know where I'll be." Lily could see how hard she was trying, and it made her angry, then guilty, then tired.

"Yes," said Lily. "I know where you are."

Arden hesitated at the front door. "I talked to Uncle Wes last night. He's coming in from Philadelphia tomorrow. We're all going to have dinner together again." Her mother's nose wrinkled as if she smelled something unpleasant. She bit her lip. "We can't do anything about your hair. But maybe you can wash and press a dress to wear?"

"I guess I can find something," Lily said.

"And could you do me one last favor?" Her mother pulled on her gloves, not looking at her. "Would you put that portrait of Uncle Max back up on the wall? Uncle Wes didn't seem to notice the last time, but I don't want to chance it again." She turned her cheek to Lily as if she expected another verbal onslaught about ghosts and all the games they play, but Lily simply nodded.

And she did as she promised—got her school clothes ready and put a couple of still-serviceable dresses in the wash. Then she went to the hall closet that had been Uncle Max's home for more than a month and took out the portrait, careful not to scratch the frame on the floor. It took only a few minutes to restore it to its place over the mantle.

Lily stepped back and took in Uncle Max's silvery blond hair, pasty face, and ghastly green eyes. His smile seemed to be wider and redder than before, but she just shrugged. He could glare all he wanted; he could throw around that stupid Kewpie doll, pant like an overheated sheepdog, explode the lightbulbs like little bombs, turn her hair blue, and it wouldn't change a thing. He was dead. Dead, dead, dead.

She put on her coat, grabbed the history books that she and Vaz had taken out of the library and never opened, and walked the ten minutes to the corner of Ocean and Hughes. Ms. Reedy was in the same spot she'd been in when Lily was there with Vaz, the raisin-hearted. Today her neckerchief was tangerine with green spots.

"Hello, Lily," she said. "I was wondering when you'd be back. Vasilios hasn't been in and I was curious about your research. How did it go at the Historical Association?"

"Uh, it didn't go," said Lily. "The guy said he was packing up to move the archive somewhere else. So, no luck."

"Oh, how disappointing for you," Ms. Reedy said.

"Not really," said Lily, who had been disappointed

so many times that she couldn't remember what it felt like not to be disappointed. "And anyway, the guy was really rude."

Ms. Reedy twisted her mouth. "Rude. Yes. He's always been rude."

"What? You know him?" Lily said.

The librarian tugged at the knot on her neckerchief, sliding it from one side of her neck to the other. "You could say that," she said. "He's my brother."

"Mr. Burton?"

"I'm afraid so."

Something clicked in her brain, and Lily looked at the nameplate on top of the counter. A. REEDY.

A. "Your last name used to be Burton," Lily said.

"Yes, before my marriage."

A.B.

M.W. + A.B.

"You knew my uncle Max," said Lily.

Ms. Reedy straightened a pile of date cards. "Excuse me?"

"I found initials carved in the attic. M.W. plus A.B. That's you, isn't it?"

"A lot of people have those initials."

"That's not an answer," said Lily. "How come you didn't tell me you were going out with my uncle Max when I was here?"

Ms. Reedy shook her head. "Why would I? That was more than forty years ago."

"You *were* going out with him, then."

"If you say so."

"Did you love him?" said Lily.

"I'm amazed that you seem to think this is your business, young lady."

"Did he love you?"

The librarian smiled without teeth, her gold eyes as inscrutable as a cat's. "Not enough, apparently, because he left me. Then again, men are terribly fickle, as I'm sure you've already discovered."

The librarian's comment hit Lily right in the gut, and she slammed the books down on the counter. "I want to return these."

Ms. Reedy flipped open the books one at a time. "Four days overdue," she said after she pulled the cards and checked the dates. "Ten cents a day per book. Three books. That adds up to a dollar twenty."

"A dollar twenty!" said Lily.

Ms. Reedy placed the cards with the red stamps on the counter facing her, pointed to the date. "Exact change is appreciated."

Lily thrust her hand inside her too-tight jeans pocket, hoping that she still had a couple of dollars. She pulled her hand out, and a couple of quarters and crumpled bills fell to the ground. She reached down to pick up the money, and she felt the silver pendant slip out from under her shirt and hit her in the chin. She stood, placing a dollar and a quarter on the counter. "There," she said.

But Ms. Reedy wasn't paying attention to the money. She was staring at Lily's pendant.

"What?" said Lily.

"Oh, nothing. I was just admiring your necklace," said Ms. Reedy. She took the money and pressed a nickel change into Lily's palm, her expression softening. "I'm sorry if I was a little . . . abrupt. There are some things I would like to forget. You'll understand when you're older."

Lily touched the pendant. "That's okay," she said.

"It's such an interesting coin."

"What is?" said Lily, looking into her palm at the nickel Ms. Reedy had just given her.

"No, not that. The coin you're wearing." Ms. Reedy pointed at the necklace.

"Coin?" Lily said. Coin! She resisted the urge to smack herself in the head. The book her mother had found in the fridge. Wasn't the book in the fridge a *coin* book?

"I'm no expert in numismatics, but I'd say that's an Indian coin. Quite old, I think. Let me show you."

Ms. Reedy walked out from behind the big front desk and led Lily to the bookshelves. She pulled out several books and leafed through them until she found a picture of what she wanted. Then she handed the book to Lily and pointed to a photo of a silver coin with markings similar to Lily's pendant.

"See?" she said. "This is a rupee from the Mogul Empire. Early to mid seventeenth century. And here's one from the late 1600s that looks very much like the coin you're wearing. The Sanskrit legends on the coin identify the ruler and the dynasty."

"Does that mean that this coin is worth a lot of money?"

"Probably not that much, but you'd have to consult a coin dealer and have it appraised," said Ms. Reedy. "May I ask where you got that piece? Is someone in the family a collector?"

"My mom found it."

"Found it, you say?" said the librarian. "How unusual." The tails of the tangerine scarf twisted in her lean hands. "One normally doesn't find rupees from the 1600s lying about."

"No," said Lily. "One doesn't." Lily knew that it was no accident that her mother had found the coin. But what did it mean? And even if it did mean something, should she care?

Lily closed the book and handed it back to Ms. Reedy. "Thanks for showing me these."

"You're quite welcome," said Ms. Reedy as they walked back to the library counter. "I can understand your curiosity about your uncle, Lily. So many terrible things have happened to your family; I would imagine it could make a person . . . tense."

"Terrible things? You mean the fire?"

"The fire, yes. So tragic. And to think Max set it himself. And the suicide," Ms. Reedy said. Then she hid her mouth with her hand. "I apologize. This is your family I'm talking about."

"Did you say suicide?"

The librarian shook her head. "This is terrible of me."

"Ms. Reedy, I didn't know any of them. Did someone else die in the house?"

The librarian heaved a great sigh, seemed— pretended?—to be struggling with herself. "Katherine Wood," she said at last. "A year after the fire, she hung herself."

Lily's skin flowered into the goose bumps that were

becoming permanent, and she asked the question she already knew the answer to. "Hung herself where?"

Ms. Reedy looked left, then right. "The chandelier," she said. "They say that she hung herself from the chandelier in the dining room."

katherine in the cradle KATHERINE IN THE CRADLE katherine in the crad

Katherine
in the Cradle

She could leave the rope, she could, but she doesn't. The rope is sweet. The rope is a brace of wind that rocks her in its cradle, the chandelier overhead an umbrella of napping stars. When she sways like this, she is clean, washed of memory. It is a kind of sleep, the swaying. She can almost feel her eyes shuddering behind her lids. Almost.

She opens her eyes and swings idly, her head tipped slightly to the left, watching the cat that watches her from the top of the dining-room table. It's a pretty cat, small and neat. She did not like cats before, but this one she likes. Its little brown boots. The way it watches. It pays attention, this cat, and Katherine, better than anyone, understands how important it is to pay attention. If she had paid more attention, perhaps things would have been different.

No, no, not that. Anything but that. She closes her eyes, tries to focus on swaying, dangling like a leaf from a tree's loving fingertip. There is peace only if she can stay clean, empty. Why can't she stay clean?

The pain wells up inside her. She squeezes her eyelids shut, but she can't stop the rush, can't erase the agony, and her mouth, once so full and red and lovely, stretches into a ring of smoke as the grief consumes her, making her buck and jerk on the end of the rope. The pretty cat moans low in its pretty throat, but she cannot console it, she cannot console herself.

Oh, my boy, my beautiful boy. What have you done?

Chapter 21

Lily gaped at the chandelier.

Her scalp tingled, and she pressed a palm to the back of her head. Someone had stroked her hair during the night—someone had left her the Kewpie. She thought it was Max, trying to haunt her or scare her or leave her another incomprehensible, creepy clue, but maybe it wasn't Max at all; maybe it was her great-grandmother Katherine, attempting to comfort her.

Were there *two* ghosts?

But even if there were, did it matter? One ghost, two ghosts, eight hundred fifty ghosts—it was all still the same. What could she do to bring peace to the dead? What could the dead do to bring peace to the living?

"Lily," her mother said, "your uncle asked if you could pass the mashed potatoes."

"Oh, sorry." She picked up the bowl of potatoes and handed it to Uncle Wes.

Uncle Wes had arrived an hour before dinner, leaving Lily to chat awkwardly with him as her mother raced around the kitchen preparing the closest thing to a feast that they could afford: a pot roast, mashed potatoes, green beans, and biscuits made from pancake mix.

"So, Lily," said Uncle Wes. "Have you started school

yet?" Lily noticed that he couldn't take his eyes off her hair, though he hadn't said anything about it. Poor Uncle Wes, appalled again.

"I start on Monday."

"That's wonderful to hear," said Uncle Wes. "Wonderful. You know how important education is to a young person. I seem to recall that your mother spent quite a bit of money sending you to the best schools, Arden." He wore a little pimple of potato on his chin.

Lily's mother worried an eyebrow with her finger. "I seem to recall that, too." She opened a bottle of wine and filled a glass almost to the brim. Her eyes looked red in the candlelight.

Uncle Wes turned to Lily. "Did your mother ever tell you about her childhood, Lily? The fine schools? The beautiful clothes? The riding and ballet lessons?"

"Some of it," said Lily.

"Your mother had the best that my family could offer her." He looked around the room. "She still does." He tore at his meat with the beautiful silverware Lily's mother had set the table with. "But what's the saying? Youth is wasted on the young? Instead of being grateful, your mother turned her back on us and chose to run off with a musician."

Lily's mother gripped her wineglass as if she were trying to crush it. "It was a long time ago."

Uncle Wes folded and refolded the napkin on his lap. "How about your job, Arden? Are you still making those trinkets of yours?"

Lily's mother blinked. "Do you mean my jewelry?"

"You know what I mean."

Her mother's eyes got flinty in a way that Lily had rarely seen. "Yes, I'm still making my trinkets. Are you still running sweatshops in Third World countries?"

"Ah," said Uncle Wes, chuckling. "There's the Arden I remember."

Arden took another sip of wine. "I'm sorry," she said. "I still get carried away sometimes."

"Of course you do," said Uncle Wes. "I wouldn't have expected anything less."

Lily could see the exhaustion, the humiliation behind her mother's clenched jaw. Lily stared down at her plate, feeling the blood rush up her neck. Now she tugged at the tight collar of the stupid old dress she wore.

"Is something bothering you, Lily?" asked Uncle Wes. "You seem uncomfortable."

Her mother gave her a look and Lily stopped wriggling. "No," she said, "I'm fine."

They ate in silence for several minutes, the only sound their forks scraping against the china. Lily noticed that Uncle Wes kept glancing up at the chandelier, too. Despite herself, she wanted to ask about his mother dying there, if he had found her, why he thought she had done it. If her great-grandmother Katherine was the sort of person who would stroke girls' hair in the middle of the night to make them feel better.

She looked at the flames atop the white dinner candles. "Why do you think Max set all those fires?"

"Lily!" said her mother.

Uncle Wes choked on his pot roast and had to sip his water. "Doing a little digging into the past?"

"Just curious," said Lily.

"So your mother has been teaching you a bit of history?"

Lily glanced at her mother and caught her beetled brows. "No. I found out on my own. At the library."

"A person can find out a lot at the library," said Uncle Wes with a tiny, almost imperceptible smirk. "If you know where to look." Lily was sure he was talking about Ms. Reedy.

"Wesley, we don't have to discuss this—" Lily's mother began, but Wes cut her off.

"No, no, Lily is interested in her family. It's understandable. So you want to know about my brother?"

"Yes," said Lily as firmly as she could with his strange mismatched gaze pinned on her. "I do want to know."

Uncle Wes patted his lips and threw the napkin next to his plate. "Maxmillian also had the best things a family could give a child. But, as with your mother, it wasn't enough for him. I was older, five, when he was born, and I knew right away that there was something strange about him. He feared nothing, wanted to try everything. Max craved excitement. When he couldn't find it climbing trees or swimming in the ocean, he read about it. He was especially fascinated with adventurers. He read about Sir Francis Bacon. Magellan. Lewis and Clark.

"He was also fascinated by criminals. That's why I wasn't surprised when he finally committed his own crime, when he set that first fire in our barn."

Lily dropped her knife to her plate with a clatter. Uncle Wes's icy blue eye passed over her. "You didn't know the fire was in our barn, did you? My mother kept our name out of the paper. She knew it was Max, you see, but she wouldn't admit it." His face hardened, darkened. "He was her favorite, her baby, her *special* boy. A dandelion from Max was like a bouquet of roses. The cheap plastic baby doll he won at a fair was like the finest antique. The next time it happened, when that boat burned in the harbor and the concession stand burned on the beach, I tried to tell her, I begged her, but she wouldn't listen."

There was a slight tinkling sound, and Lily looked up to see some of the crystals on the chandelier brushing against one another, like a wind chime in a summer breeze.

Lost in the past, Uncle Wes did not seem to hear. "Then came the fire on the third floor, in his bedroom. No one knows why he did it. I don't suppose there is a reason. Max just wanted to see what would happen. But we'd always had a problem with his door sticking. Max set that fire and then couldn't escape. By the time we smelled the smoke downstairs, he was dead."

Lily shivered involuntarily, still eyeing the chandelier. "What about your mother?"

Uncle Wes gave her an empty smile. "You read about that, too?" Lily nodded.

"She blamed herself." He stood, agitated. "She blamed herself and she hung herself. From there." He pointed at the light fixture arching above them.

The phone shattered the ensuing silence. Nobody moved until Uncle Wes said, "Well? Is anyone going to answer that?"

Lily stood quickly and went to the phone. "Hello?"

"Lily!" Vaz said. "I've been calling you for days!"

She didn't know whether to be relieved or furious. She chose furious. "Look, I'm busy right now."

"You've been busy forever. What's going on?"

"You tell me."

"I don't know what you're talking about."

"Sure you do. She's short and blond."

"What? Who?"

"Forget it."

"I'm coming over," said Vaz.

"You can't," said Lily, glancing into the dining room. "My uncle Wes is here."

"He is! Did you tell him about the ghosts?"

"None of your business."

"I'm definitely coming over," he said.

"I'm hanging up."

"Wait! Remember that model we found in Burton's library? The *Quedah Merchant*? I looked it up. Guess what it is?"

"I have no idea."

"Captain Kidd's ship."

Her brain screamed, but she kept her tone cool. "So?"

"So! It's a pirate ship, Lily. What do pirate ships carry?"

Lily made a face at the receiver and put it back in the cradle. Then she walked back into the dining room and sat.

"A friend of yours?" said Uncle Wes.

"No," she said. Ship! In the reading at the Good Fortunes Shoppe, Max had tried to tell her about a ship. Was it Captain Kidd's ship? She put a hand to her throat, under her collar, to check to see if her pendant was still there. What if the coin was a part of some sort of treasure? What if that was what Uncle Max wanted her to find?

"What are you doing?" Uncle Wes said, staring at her neck.

Lily dropped her hand to her lap. "Nothing."

"You have something around your neck."

"So she's wearing a necklace, Wes. What's the matter?" said Lily's mother.

"What *kind* of necklace? Let me see it."

"It's no big deal," said Lily.

"Let me see it!" Uncle Wes yelled.

"Show him, Lily," said her mother, her face a mask of worry.

Reluctantly Lily pulled the chain from beneath her collar. Uncle Wes's green eye looked almost yellow, like a snake's. "Where did you get that?" he hissed.

"Nowhere," said Lily. "Mom found it."

"Where did you get it?" Before she knew what was happening, Uncle Wes had lifted her out of the chair by her shoulders.

"What are you doing?" her mother said. "Let her go!"

Wes ignored her, shaking Lily like a rag doll as her mother pulled at his arm. "You tell me where it is!"

Lily was so surprised at his actions, at the strength of his grip, she could only gasp, "Where *what* is?"

He grabbed the silver coin and yanked the necklace from her neck. "The rest of it!"

The doorbell rang. Uncle Wes, still holding the necklace, shoved her away. "Answer the door," he said coldly.

In shock, Lily shuffled to the door like a robot. She heard her mother behind her: "Wesley, have you gone crazy? What's the matter with you?"

Lily opened the door. It was Bailey Burton gazing up at her, a predatory gleam in his piggy eyes.

A smile cut into the moist, doughy face. "I hope I'm not too late for dinner."

Chapter 22

Bailey Burton followed Lily back to the dining room, his hand around the back of her neck.

"What took you so long?" said Wesley.

"What in the hell is going on here?" Lily's mother said.

Wesley sighed. "Stop swearing, Arden, please. You sound about as low class as they come. And sit down."

"Get your hands off my daughter!"

"Let go of her, Burton," said Wesley. Bailey Burton let go of her and Lily went to stand by her mother, rubbing her neck. "I'm sorry, Lily. We're just a little excited."

Lily scowled at him. No one had ever grabbed her like that before, and she was surprised at how angry she was. She wanted to punch someone.

"Now, where were we?" said Wesley. "Ah, the treasure. You were about to tell me where it is."

Bailey grabbed the bowl of green beans and popped one into his mouth. Then another.

Lily licked her lips. "I don't know what you're talking about."

"Don't lie, little girl," Wesley spat. "We know what you've been doing. Your little investigation? Tsk, tsk, tsk. Did you know breaking and entering is a serious charge?"

He thrust the necklace in her face. "Where did you get this?"

"I gave it to her," said Lily's mother.

Wesley's eyes narrowed. "I knew it," he said. "I knew that's why you were here. I knew you could lead us to it." He paced the floor as Lily and her mother exchanged glances.

Wesley pointed at Lily's mother. "Where's the rest of it?"

"The rest of what?"

"The coins! The coins!"

Lily's mother tossed her curly hair and looked at Wesley as if he had completely lost his mind. "That's it," she said. "I only found the one coin. The cat was playing with it. I don't know where she found it."

"Liar!" barked Wesley. "I know you came here to claim it."

Lily's mother gazed at him. "We only came here to get back on our feet."

"Then why did the child talk about being rich when you can barely afford to clothe her?"

Lily's mother took a deep breath. "She always says things like that. It . . . hasn't been easy for her. I haven't made it easy for her." She looked sadly at Lily.

"Stories! You refused the money when I offered it."

"What does that prove? When was the last time I took money from you?" said Lily's mother. "From anyone?"

Wesley stared at her, hard, but as there was nothing but confusion and anger on her face, he seemed to relax. He sat down at the dining-room table and reached into his jacket, pulling out an engraved silver case and a lighter. Without taking his eyes off Lily and her mother, he lit a slim brown cigar and took a few deep drags.

"Terrible habit," he said. "Gives me horrific sinus problems, but I can't stop."

Lily stared at him. He was crazy. She wished Vaz would come. Maybe he had picked up some karate in junior high.

"Sit down at the table, Lily," Wesley said. "Go on." Bailey Burton pushed her forward, and she sat, facing her uncle.

He put the necklace on the table, nudged it to her with a fingertip. "You know what that is, don't you?"

Lily didn't look at the coin. "Yes," she said. "It's an Indian rupee. It's very old."

"That it is," said Wes. "I told you that my dear brother liked to read of the exploits of adventurers and criminals. There was one in particular that caught his attention. Do you know who it might be?"

"No," said Lily.

"William Kidd. Captain William Kidd. Have you ever heard of him, Lily?"

Lily nodded slowly.

"Of course you have. And do you remember what Captain Kidd was famous for?"

"He was a pirate." Bailey reached around her and grabbed a couple of biscuits. She could hear the dry scrape of his teeth against the bread.

"Clever girl," said Wesley. "As I was saying, my brother was particularly interested in the story of Captain Kidd, a man who began his career as a privateer—that's a person who has been given permission by his government to legally plunder the ships of other countries—and ended it swinging from a rope." He blew a ring of smoke. "It *is* a fascinating story. And you can't imagine how excited my brother became when he read of Captain Kidd's last voyage."

Uncle Wesley stood and moved around to the opposite side of the table, as if it were a lectern and he a professor. "It seems that in the beginning of 1698, Captain Kidd managed to capture a ship, the *Quedah Merchant*, while prowling the Indian Ocean."

Bailey squeezed Lily's shoulder. "You remember the *Quedah Merchant*, don't you? You and your *friend* left your greasy fingerprints all over it."

"Down, Burton," said Wesley. "Let me finish. Now, the *Quedah* was a huge prize, a four-hundred-ton ship carrying silk, muslin, calico, sugar, opium, and other goods. Kidd sailed it to Caliquilon, a city on the southern tip of India, and immediately sold most of the cargo. But that's not the most interesting part of the story. The most interesting part is what happened after the *Quedah Merchant* crossed the Atlantic and Kidd exchanged it for a sloop called the *Saint Antonio* and set sail up the U.S. coast."

Lily twitched in her chair. "Where did he sail to?"

"Ah, a good question. Don't you think that's an excellent question, Arden?"

Lily's mother didn't move a muscle as Wesley put both hands on the table and leaned forward toward Lily.

"Some say that he hit landfall somewhere in the lower Delaware Bay, then proceeded on to Long Island, where he buried some of his treasure. Others have it that he landed on the bay side at Cape May Point and buried his treasure there." He stubbed out his cigar in the mashed potatoes, though he'd smoked only half. Bailey, who was reaching for the potatoes, looked upset.

"Have you ever been to Cape May Point, Lily?" Wesley asked.

"No."

"No?" Again he made the tsk, tsk sound with his tongue. "It's quite beautiful. An old lighthouse, a bird sanctuary. A lake, too. It's called Lake Lily, can you imagine? What a coincidence! Unfortunately, the lake is dying. Apparently there's some sort of nutrient build-up. A shame."

He laughed, reached for another cigar, lit it. "For over three hundred years, people have been looking for Captain Kidd's treasure on Cape May Point. If he had buried it there, I'm sure someone would have found it by now."

"But he didn't bury it there," said Lily.

"No, you clever, clever girl. He didn't bury it there. He buried it somewhere else. My brother found it. You have a piece of that treasure in front of you."

"You're kidding," said Lily's mother, her words almost a snicker.

"No pun intended, I assume?" said Wesley. "No, I'm quite serious, Arden." He walked around the table and sat in the chair next to Lily, turning it to face her. "And

215

I would very much like to speak seriously with you, Lily."

"I thought we were."

"What a delightful little fox of a girl!" said Wesley. "Burton, wouldn't you say that she's a clever little fox?"

"A beautiful pink fox." Bailey's hot breath churned in her ear, and Lily longed to shrink away. Where was Vaz? Where was Max?

"Maxmillian made a map before he succumbed to his own sick passion for crime. A treasure map. I know, because he taunted me with it before he hid it away. He enjoyed taunting me. He was very ill. Exceedingly ill. Did you see the portrait on the wall in the TV room? Then you understand how sick he was. I had that portrait commissioned after he died."

"Well, that explains why it looks that way," said Lily's mother.

Wesley spat a cloud of smoke. "I let you stay here because I knew you could lead me to the map. We know you've been looking for something. Mr. Burton's been keeping an eye on you for some time. He's seen you running around your yard with that boy, and he knows you've been searching his library."

"And digging on the beach," said Bailey, in a cloud of coppery breath. "I have a powerful telescope. And I read lips."

"He reads lips!" Wesley said.

"Hit the road, Odysseus!" Bailey Burton hissed.

"His idea of a joke, though I had to ask him to refrain from any others. An unusual talent, Bailey Burton is. So

I need to ask you, you sneaky little fox of a thing. *Where is the map?*"

Lily opened her mouth to speak, to tell him that she didn't know what he was talking about, to tell him that he was crazy, to tell her mother to call the police, when the doorbell set to cheeping like an irritated parakeet.

Wesley straightened with a snap. "Who could that be?"

Chapter 23

Wesley jerked his chin in Bailey's direction. "Get rid of whoever it is," he said. "Make it quick."

Bailey trudged off obediently. They heard the door open and Bailey say, "What are you doing here? You can't come in here!"

Footsteps coming closer. Wesley scooped the necklace from the table and shoved it in his pocket.

"Well, it looks like a regular party," said Ms. Reedy, dragging Vaz into the dining room by the elbow. She was wearing a plush, shiny fur coat and fire-engine-red lipstick against which her teeth glinted like pearls. "I found this one lurking around the windows. I'm surprised that you weren't looking out for him, considering how much time these two have spent together. Then again, I suspect they might be having a lovers' spat. The little girl came to see me alone today."

Bailey grabbed Vaz and sat him down in one of the dining-room chairs. Vaz looked around wildly, the crazy curl on his forehead standing at attention. He stared at Ms. Reedy as if he'd never seen her before, then he turned and gazed at Lily, his big eyes getting even bigger.

"Lily," he said. "What happened to your hair? What's

going on?" He pointed at Ms. Reedy and shook his head in amazement.

"Aurelia," said Wesley warily.

"Wesley," said Ms. Reedy. Feeling Lily's stare, she smiled. "Hello, Lily. I meant to ask you earlier, an accident at the salon?" Then she saw Lily's mother. "And you must be Arden. It's lovely to meet you."

She removed the fur, unveiling a slim-cut red dress that perfectly matched her lipstick, and tall black boots with an elegant heel. She looked as if she'd just walked off a movie set. "So!" she said, rubbing her hands together. "What have we discovered here tonight?"

"I don't think this is any of your business," Bailey Burton began, jowls quivering. "I think you should go."

"Is that any way to talk to family?"

"As you can see, Aurelia, we're a bit busy," said Wesley. "Perhaps if you come back another time?"

"Let's skip the nonsense, shall we?" said Ms. Reedy. "I saw the girl wearing the coin."

"She doesn't even know where it is," Bailey grumbled.

"Shut up, Burton!" Wesley said.

"Of course she knows where it is!" the woman said. "You're just not asking her the right questions."

"Oh?" said Wesley. "And which questions would you ask?"

Ms. Reedy shooed Wesley from the seat next to Lily and sat there herself. "You must ignore him. As you can see, he's a bit overzealous. It's probably all his financial troubles. It turns out his mother may have been correct in assuming that his was not a head for business after all."

"I wouldn't, Aurelia," Wesley snarled.

"Quiet," said Ms. Reedy. "Wesley, do you want to know where the map is or don't you?"

"Of course I do."

"Then let me handle this, hmmm?"

Wesley backed away, muttering to himself, and Ms. Reedy turned her attention back to Lily, patting her hand. Emphasized by the red color, Ms. Reedy's lips were full and lush, and Lily couldn't keep her eyes off them. It was like there were two Ms. Reedys—the staid librarian and her sexy twin.

"I've known Wesley for some years now. And I can tell you firsthand that he has a lot of pride. That pride often keeps him from telling the whole story."

Ms. Reedy picked up one of the forks from the table. "You can see by the fine things in the house that your uncle's family was quite wealthy. When Wesley's father died, your great-grandmother Katherine took over the family's businesses." She picked at the fork tines with a red fingernail. "The Woods had holdings everywhere . . . manufacturing, retail, and so forth. Naturally these holdings would eventually go to one of her children, and naturally most assumed that Wesley would be chosen to take over the family's interests as soon as he was old enough."

She held up the fork. "Alas, poor Wesley. Even simple math was a challenge. Isn't that right?"

Wesley grunted in wordless fury, chewing on the tip of his cigar.

"Ruth was already married, and a girl besides, so

Katherine pinned her hopes on Max. She had to ignore all the signs of his . . . er . . . troubles, of course, but no one could deny that Max was incredibly bright."

Lily found her voice to ask the question Ms. Reedy hadn't bothered to answer back in the library. "Did you love him?"

Bailey Burton snorted. Ms. Reedy blinked slowly, and Lily thought that, for just one moment, the woman looked pained. "He was special."

"He was insane," said Wesley. "He thought he could talk to ghosts."

Lily glanced at Vaz. Ms. Reedy took note. "It's true. As a matter of fact, that's how he claimed he knew where the treasure was buried. He said he'd seen the ghost of Captain Kidd on the beach."

She peered at Lily through the tines in the fork. "Max was eccentric, but he loved his mother. When he found out that Wesley was more than a little interested in his pirate treasure, he hid the map. For his mother, he said. But the fool set that fire before he had the chance to tell his mother *where* he'd hidden it. And then Katherine killed herself."

"The bastard broke her heart. I always said he couldn't be trusted," Wesley said.

"So you keep telling us." Ms. Reedy put the fork on the table. "Obviously Wesley searched the house top to bottom and found nothing. We can only conclude that wherever the map was hidden, it was hidden in something that perhaps Katherine unwittingly gave away? To your grandmother Ruth perhaps?"

Lily's mother spoke up. "My mother never said anything about any of this. Never."

"You didn't speak to her for years," Uncle Wes said.

A smile played about Ms. Reedy's red mouth as she gazed at Lily's mother. "Think about it. Did she leave you anything, perhaps?" She shot a hard look at Wes. "*That's* the question you should have asked."

All throughout the evening, Lily's mind had been racing from one thing to the next like a crazed chipmunk, thought to thought, idea to idea, never stopping on any particular thing. But now her brain had screeched to a halt, zeroed in on a single picture.

Lily saw Ms. Reedy's slow, languid smile and knew the knowledge was all over her face, as surely as if it had been scrawled on her skin with the librarian's shocking red lipstick. "You know where it is, don't you, Lily?"

Wesley took two large steps and leaned into Lily's face. "Tell me," he said.

"I think I've had just about enough," said Lily's mother, standing. "I think it's about time I called the police." Vaz leaped to his feet.

Wesley reached into his jacket and pulled out a small silver gun. "Sit down, both of you."

"Wesley!" Lily's mother said, the color draining from her face. "What are you doing?"

"I said sit!" Arden sat.

Ms. Reedy looked up at Wesley, frowning. "Really, Wesley, must you—"

"I must, Aurelia," Wesley said, backing up and turning the gun on her. "I suggest that no one move too quickly."

He swung the gun around to Vaz, who looked more interested in throttling someone than in sitting down. "You!" Wesley barked. "No heroics from you."

Vaz's eyes got small and squinty, and Lily could see a muscle tighten in his jaw as he sat back down.

Then Wesley turned the gun on Lily. She gripped the arms of the chair and pressed her lips together to keep them from trembling as she looked at the small black hole. He wouldn't shoot her, would he? Was he that crazy?

"Now," he said. "Where is the map?"

"The doll," Lily said quickly. "It's in the doll."

"What doll?" said Wesley. "Where?"

"My room, the first bedroom on the left," Lily said. "It was my grandmother's. A Kewpie doll in a red dress."

"Go get it," Wesley said to Bailey. "Now." Bailey turned and hurried out of the room.

Ms. Reedy watched her brother leave, and Lily thought that she saw worry lines furrowing her skin. Why was she worried? Wasn't she getting exactly what she wanted?

Ms. Reedy met Lily's eyes, and the worry lines smoothed out as if they'd never been there at all. "You want to know why I'm here."

Lily lifted her chin, speechless with rage and fear and confusion.

Ms. Reedy shrugged. "It's true he was a little odd. He was so absentminded, his mother would sometimes find his books in the icebox. But I had grown up with nothing, and he was heir to a fortune. And then he found the treasure that people had been seeking for more than three hundred years. We would have been set for life. Our children and our children's children would have been set for life. If he hadn't gone and gotten himself killed.

"I married a schoolteacher who left me a widow at thirty. Since then, I've been working as a librarian, the steward of the treasures of history. After all that I've been through, it seems right, almost poetic, that I should be the steward of any literal treasures left here."

"What do you mean, *you* should be the steward?" said Wesley. "This is my treasure, Aurelia."

"Our treasure," Ms. Reedy said. "Yours and mine and Bailey's."

Wesley waved the gun. "Aurelia, I'm warning you—"

The sadness on Ms. Reedy's face fled, and her expression hardened. "Oh, Wesley, don't waste my time with threats. If anything happens to me, if I don't call in by midnight tonight, my lawyer has instructions to alert the authorities. I'm sure you don't want the authorities involved, do you? Who do you think would get the treasure then? The state of New Jersey, perhaps? The federal government?"

Wesley clutched the gun tighter, but Ms. Reedy turned back to Lily.

"So you ruined the microfilm at the library?" Lily asked.

Ms. Reedy tugged her neckerchief. "Of course not. There's nothing in those papers about the treasure. And besides, no one is interested in history. Except for you, Lily. And my dear brother, of course, and he's too stingy to share. That's why I sent you and Vasilios to Bailey's house."

"How did you know what we were looking for?"

"I wasn't sure until you came in wearing that necklace. After all these years, I couldn't believe that I might have a chance to find it."

Just then Bailey returned, holding the Kewpie in his hands. As they watched, he grabbed the doll's head in one of his hands, yanked it off, and tossed it to the floor.

"Oh, dear," said Ms. Reedy. "Why don't you simply look in the clothing?"

Bailey scowled and picked at the buttons. He slid a finger down the back of the red dress and found a yellowed piece of paper pinned to the inside. Lily's mother gasped. Bailey carefully removed the paper. "This is it," he said, his Halloween face cracking into a smile.

"Wonderful," said Ms. Reedy. "Well, it's time to get moving then." She eyed Arden. "Tie her up," she said. "I have a feeling that she could give us some trouble."

Bailey pointed at Vaz. "What about that one?"

"He comes with us. Both of them do," said Wesley.

"I hardly think we need—" began Ms. Reedy.

"Enough, Aurelia, you've had your fun. It's my show now. They can dig while we keep an eye on them."

"Please don't do this, Wesley," said Lily's mother.

Lily could barely keep herself from breaking out into sobs as Wesley hauled Vaz to his feet, as she watched Bailey Burton lash her mother's hands and feet to the dining-room chair, stuff a linen napkin into her mouth. She felt a stiff, frigid breeze, smelled the sharp tang of smoke, and yearned for Max to do something, anything. Why wasn't he helping?

Wesley pointed to the map. "Max actually measured everything off in paces! And there's nothing here but a circle marked WELCOME. How do we know where we're supposed to start pacing from?"

Ms. Reedy rolled her eyes. "Men," she said to Lily, "are braggarts, deceivers, and idiots. It would do you well to remember that." To Wesley she said, "*Here*. We begin right here in this house, at the front door." She slid into her fur coat. "Good-bye, Arden. I hope you're not too uncomfortable."

Lily saw a single tear streaking down her mother's face before Wesley poked the gun into Lily's back and ordered her to get moving.

Chapter 24

With Vaz and Lily in front, Bailey, Wesley, and Ms. Reedy behind, the group paced one hundred ninety-seven steps from the front door to the first street lamp at the Congress Hotel (marked GOVERNMENT on the map).

"They could have moved the street lamp since 1953," said Wesley.

"Trust me, they didn't. The preservationists would have had a fit," said Ms. Reedy.

The sidewalk next to the hotel was blocked off. "Now what do we do?" whined Bailey.

"Walk in the street," Wesley said. "And stop whining. You sound like a child."

Two hundred twenty more steps and they reached the street pole marking Beach Drive. They paced across the street until they hit the sidewalk. Another turn, right, and they paced to the promenade. Five steps up, five steps over, five steps down to the beach.

"What now?" said Bailey.

"One hundred sixty-one paces southeast."

"Couldn't he have just started at the beach?" Bailey said. "We didn't need to count all the way down here."

Wesley snorted. "My brother loved to waste other people's time."

"Stop," said Ms. Reedy. She removed a compass from the folds of her voluminous coat, the markings on the gadget luminescent in the dark. She pointed. "That way. Let the boy count it off; he's about the right size." She pushed Vaz ahead. He looked back at Lily. Ms. Reedy shook her head. "You can gaze into each other's eyes later. Now walk."

Vaz counted off the paces while the rest of them followed, Ms. Reedy keeping them on a precise course. The night was dark and moonless, the inky sky streaked with ashen clouds. Lily shivered in her thin dress and coat, felt the sand creeping into her shoes and stockings as they walked. The sound of the surf crashing into the beach got louder and louder. She couldn't see how they were going to get out of this.

"One fifty-nine, one sixty, one sixty-one." Vaz stopped walking.

Wesley handed a shovel to Vaz and one to Lily. "Dig," he said. "And put your backs into it."

Vaz and Lily started to dig. The dry sand on top wasn't too heavy, but soon they reached the wet sand underneath. Lily began to sweat, the skin on her hands burning. After what seemed to be hours and hours, the hole now several feet deep, Lily stopped to flex her aching, blistered fingers.

"Did you hear a whistle? Did anyone say it was break time?" said Wesley.

Lily risked a glare, but she picked up the shovel and continued her digging. Her back and arms were on fire. She could hear Vaz grunting as he lifted each shovelful, could see the sweat dampening his dark curls. He glanced up at Lily, throwing a load of wet sand behind him. "She's just a friend," he said.

"The drama of young love," said Ms. Reedy, her voice chilly. "I'm glad those days are over for me."

Lily ignored her and tightened her grip on the shovel. "It doesn't matter."

He threw another load of sand over his shoulder. "Yes, it does. Kami's a good friend."

"You like her. I could see it that day at the library."

Vaz grunted as he dug. "Okay. I did like her. Sort of. But then I got to know you."

Lily jammed her shovel into the sand and stepped on it. Tears stung her cheeks, her own hair whipping across her face to rake them away. She couldn't trust her own instincts or her own judgment; no matter what she thought, she always seemed to get it backward or inside out or wrong. He had come when she needed him, and now they were here, digging themselves deeper, together. That meant something, didn't it? She did not know what would happen to them if they found the treasure, or if they didn't.

Vaz was right. It mattered.

Lily nodded. "Just a friend. Okay."

"Shut up and dig," barked Wesley, angling the gun so they could see it.

They dug.

The hole was nearly five feet deep when Lily hit something with her shovel. Ms. Reedy must have heard the muffled *whump*, because her face appeared over the edge. "What was that?"

"I don't know," said Lily.

"Well, find out, you silly girl!" Wesley said.

The two of them got to their knees and used their hands to dig at the sand. Soon the top of a small leather trunk was visible. Lily couldn't help but feel excited at the sight of it.

"Get it out," said Wesley as they stood and started digging around the edge of the trunk to free it from the heavy sand. It took another half hour before they could heft the leaden weight out of the hole and hand it up to Wesley and Bailey. They were both panting with exhaustion as they crawled out of the hole.

Bailey leaped on the trunk, yanking at the ancient lock, but Uncle Wes stopped him. "Wait," he said. "Let me savor the moment with a smoke."

Ms. Reedy looked on in disgust. "Really, Wesley!"

"Aurelia. Let me enjoy this."

Bailey's eyes looked like they were going to burst from his face, but Ms. Reedy threw up her hands. "Oh, Bailey, let the man have his fun. We've waited more than forty years. What's another minute?"

Still holding the gun, Uncle Wes reached into his jacket pocket, pulled out a cigar, and placed it in the corner of his mouth. Then he pulled out his lighter and flicked it open with his thumb. The flame was tall, bluish, ghostly in the dark. As Lily watched, he dialed the flame higher and brighter, his watery eyes glittering behind it. The tip of his tongue darted against his livery lips. His eyes caressed the flame, and Lily remembered him insisting on setting the fire himself that first evening at the house, remembered him saying that fire was "one of man's greatest inventions."

It was then that Lily knew that Max hadn't set those fires. Wesley had. She imagined Uncle Wes dragging an unconscious Max to a corner of a dark room, striking a match, locking the door. Leaving his brother to die.

Lily gripped the shovel so hard she thought the skin on her hands would split. She glanced at Bailey Burton and Ms. Reedy, both waiting impatiently for Wesley to finish his heinous little ritual. They were both at least sixty years old. She was sure that Vaz could take them if he had to. It was the gun, and Wesley, she was worried about. If she could just knock it from his hands.

Now, her mind prodded her, *while he's still distracted.*

She lifted the shovel just as Wesley turned. She heard Vaz shout, "Lily!" just as Wesley brought the gun down on the side of her head. Fireworks fizzled in her brainpan, and then there was nothing.

hosts GHOSTS ghosts GHOSTS ghosts GHOSTS ghosts GHOSTS ghosts GHOS

Ghosts

h e seemed to be floating beside her, skin so pale it was
nearly blue. She gazed at him in wonder. "Hello, Max."
    "Hello, Lily."

"Your hands are on fire."

He shrugged. "They're always like that. I'm used to it."

She looked around. She could see a swirling gray mist with
shadows shifting behind it, like people passing behind a gauze
curtain. "Am I dead?"

"No," he said. He danced in the sand. "You're dreaming."

"I don't think so. It usually doesn't hurt this much when I
dream."

"Then you must be dead." He stopped dancing. "What does
it feel like, dreaming?" he asked. "I forget."

"Dreaming feels real, mostly," said Lily.

"Oh," he said. "I forget how that feels, too."

"I'm sorry I didn't believe in you at first. I wasn't sure if *you*
were real."

"And now you're sure?"

Lily frowned. "Well, I can see you. And I can touch . . ." She
reached out, but Max drew back.

"Does your mother love you?" he asked.

"Of course," said Lily. "What does that have to do with anything?"

235

"How do you know that she loves you, if you can't see love? If you can't touch it?"

Even with the fog in her head and the fog swirling about her, Lily was annoyed. "You've been trying to tell me something. But I didn't understand."

"We often don't understand what's important."

"Max, you put jam in my shoes," said Lily. "What was that supposed to mean?"

Max laughed, the sound like the leaves rustling in the trees. "That wasn't me."

"Who was it? Katherine?"

"A spiteful soul bent on mischief." In the air, he traced a name in fire: LOLA. "She'll be here a long time."

"Where's here?"

Max closed his eyes. "Nowhere."

Lily was suddenly frightened. "Isn't there a heaven?"

"Heavens, yes. Many heavens."

"Why aren't you in heaven, then?"

"We are earthbound until we learn. Some learn while alive, others learn while dead, a few never learn."

"What did you have to learn?"

"Compassion." He shook his head sadly. "The hardest thing to learn."

"I don't understand," Lily said. "Wesley murdered you, didn't he? Isn't this all to avenge your murder?"

"Oh, I've already seen to that."

"What do you mean?"

Max's smile was serene. "Our worlds collect and the skin between them thins, so that even the dead can see. It will all soon be over."

"What will be over?"

But Max just danced his strange, loping dance, and Lily got tired of watching him. "Where's Katherine?"

"At the house. She doesn't like to leave the house. She likes to hang in the dining room. She says it makes her feel clean. It helps her forget." Max twirled in a circle, so fast that it made Lily's head spin more than it was already. "You made her remember. You and your mother. She gave you the doll. You kept giving it back."

"I didn't know what the doll meant."

"You still don't. You'll have to open the trunk to find out."

"Isn't the treasure in there?"

"A treasure, yes. But only in the eyes of some."

"Was Ms. Reedy right? Did you really talk to Captain Kidd?"

"All the time. He lets me wear his hat. It has a feather in it. We made a deal, he and I."

Lily was confused again. She was always confused. "About the treasure? You made a deal about the treasure?"

"Treasure isn't everything. It's not even that much of something. There's love and kindness and hope and art. That, and dreams. People need to dream, or else they die."

"My mother said that! You're quoting her!"

"Are you sure?"

"Well, no," said Lily. "I'm not sure of anything right now."

"That's because you're dead. The dead are never sure."

"Then I don't want to be dead anymore."

"Uh-oh. You're going to have to—"

"Wake up!" shrieked the woman in the flowered bathing cap.

"Uh? Wha'?" said the man. He sat up on his elbows. He was wearing purple eye shadow and what little hair he had on his head was gathered into dozens of tiny braids, making his head appear like the body of a strange, many-legged insect.

"Get away from him, you hoodlum!" said the woman, hitting out with her straw bag at the girl in the fuchsia satin skirt.

The girl backed away, cackled. "Oh, come on! I was just having a little fun." She smiled at the man. "You don't mind, do you?"

The woman looked past the hoodlum and gasped. She clutched at her husband's arm. "The little girl who built those castles! That man just hit her with something!"

"What?" said the hoodlum, whirling to look behind her. "Hey! I know her! I know that guy, too!"

The woman wailed, "Why did he have to hit her? What kind of monster is he?"

"Quiet, both of you," hissed the man, scrambling to stand and shoving his blue feet into his sandals. "You don't know what's going on over there right now. I say we get outta here before they see us."

"Oh! Now they're attacking that poor old lady!" the woman said. As the three of them watched, the short, wormy man with the big head wrapped his arms around the teenage boy to subdue him. The older woman in the fur coat wrestled awkwardly with the other man.

The wife looked around at the beach, packed with folks of all shapes and sizes, a scant few watching the strange people who had forced the children to dig a large hole, most going about their business. "Why isn't anyone doing something to help? Why are they acting like everything is normal? What's wrong with everyone?"

"Keep it down, will ya?" yelled the man, who subsequently

realized *he* wasn't keeping it down and threw a look of pure terror at the group gathered around the hole. None of them seemed to hear. One of them, the gaunt man, was screaming at the teenaged boy, telling him to sit down and shut up.

The woman stood, flowered bathing cap quivering in fury. "If you're not going to do anything, I am!"

The girl in fishnets crossed her arms. "No way. Really?" She seemed to think a minute. "I'm coming, too. I mean, what the heck, right? Heart's what it's all about."

"For god's sake, will you both can it! That's crazy talk!"

But his wife had already grabbed the striped bedsheet they had been using as a blanket and was marching over to the strange people, the girl close behind. Any minute and they were going to turn around and see a two-hundred-pound woman in a polka-dotted swimsuit brandishing a fitted queen-size sheet, and a teenage girl in a cancan costume. And then they'd be done for.

He saw a large tin bucket filled with plastic sand toys in a net bag, and he swiped the bucket as he lumbered after them.

"Jesus Christ in a red pickup truck," he said. "We're *all* done for."

Chapter 25

"Wake up, Lily! Come on, wake up!"

She tried to lift her head, but it weighed so much. The left side of her face rang with pain; her cheek felt as if it were broken. Was that possible? Can a person break a cheek?

"Come on, Lily, can you hear me?"

"Get away from her and sit down, boy! You, too, Aurelia!" a terrible voice said.

"Max?" said Lily. "Where are you?"

"Uh-oh, Wesley," a man said. "You've given her brain damage."

"She's lucky then. I could have shot her." It was the terrible voice again. She hated the voice. She wished someone would make it shut up.

"Shut up," she said.

Another voice, whining. "The girl had a shovel, Aurelia. She was going to hit him."

"She should have," the woman said, in a voice that sounded like a snakebite. They were all terrible voices.

Lily opened up one eye, and Vaz's anxious face floated above hers. "Vaz?" she whispered. "What happened?"

Vaz jerked his head in Wes's direction, his eyes hard with fury. "*He* hit you with the butt of the gun. He hit *her* when she tried to get the gun away from him."

Lily turned her head and saw Ms. Reedy crouched in the sand next to her, cradling her own cheek. "I'm sorry," the librarian said. Her red lipstick was smeared across her chin, making her skin look burned in the moonlight. "I thought the gun was just more of Wesley's bluster. I never thought he would hurt you."

"Vaz," said Lily. "Where's Max?"

Her uncle Wes's jarring eyes appeared next to Vaz's. "Dead," he said. "Max is dead."

"You killed him," Lily said, struggling to sit up, one hand on her possibly broken cheek. "You killed your own brother."

Ms. Reedy gasped. *"What?"*

"I think that bump on the head addled your brains," said Bailey Burton. "Max killed himself."

"He didn't," said Lily, struggling to speak through the ringing in her head. "Wesley did. He set all the fires and tried to blame them on Max. But your mother didn't believe it, did she? She suspected you." Despite the pain, Lily's mind was clear. "That's why Katherine hung herself."

"This can't be true," said Ms. Reedy. "It can't."

Wesley plucked the cigar from his mouth and threw it to the sand. "You're a filthy little monkey. You'll do your mother proud." He strode over to the trunk, gesturing to his companions. "Let's open this up."

Bailey Burton hesitated. "Is it true, Wesley?"

Wesley's eyes narrowed. "What is it, Burton? All of a sudden you have a conscience?" He looked at Ms. Reedy, who had clapped both hands over her mouth, tears running over them. "And you, too, Aurelia? You, who would have jilted my poor besotted brother in a hot minute if a richer man had come along? You, who told us about the treasure when he wasn't even cold in his grave?"

"No, no, no." Ms. Reedy dropped her hands, her face knotted with anguish. "All this time, I thought he'd left me. All this time, I thought he didn't love me. I've been such a fool. A venal, silly fool."

"You'll get no argument from me," said Wes.

"He was your brother, Wesley," Ms. Reedy spat. "Your own brother. How could you? How could you hurt him like that?"

"Somebody always gets hurt," said Wesley. "It's the way of the world."

"Max, Max," Ms. Reedy moaned, "I'm so sorry." She ripped the cranberry scarf from her neck and struggled to her feet. "I may be a fool, but I'm not a murderer. I won't let you do this."

Wesley looked down his nose at her as if she were about as threatening as a moth. "You're more arrogant than my brother was. He tried to stop me, too." Wesley turned to Bailey Burton.

"I hope you're not crazy, Burton. I hope you can get yourself together and remember why we're all here," he said. "Now are you going to help me open this damned trunk, or do I have to take all the treasure for myself?"

Bailey took a few steps forward. "All right, no need to get hot under the collar." Suddenly he stopped in mid-stride, flailing his arms and tugging at his face. "Hey!" he shouted. "Hey!" He danced around blindly, though

Lily could see that his eyes were open. His arms were stretched out in front of him like a mummy in a horror movie. "Wesley! Help!"

"What's wrong with him?" said Ms. Reedy.

"I don't know," said Vaz. "It's like somebody threw a blanket over his head."

Wesley backed up a few steps, waving the gun, but Bailey kept up his blind charge. His screams suddenly became strangely muffled. "Get it off me!" he cried. He held his hands to his head but didn't actually touch his skin, like there was an invisible helmet between his head and his hands. His head abruptly pitched sideways, as if it were a gong and an invisible someone was ringing it. "Stop it, stop it, stop!" His cry was a deadened moaning sound, like a voice over an intercom. "Stop it!"

Vaz put his leg out, tripping the man, and Bailey fell to the ground and banged his head into the sand.

Wesley watched in horror. He ran to Lily and hauled her to her feet, shoved the gun under her chin. "Make him stop."

"What?" said Lily. She knew she should be terrified of the gun, but she was just plain mad. "Stop who?"

"Max!" he screamed. "Make him stop!"

"Max?" she said. "Max is doing this?"

Just then a furious yell ripped through the air, and they turned to see Lily's mother sprinting toward them across the sand, looking like some kind of angry priestess.

Wesley pulled the gun from Lily's neck and pointed it at Arden, but Arden kept coming, her face contorted in maternal rage.

"Mom! Stop!" Lily screamed.

Vaz kicked out and knocked the gun from Wesley's hand. Lily picked up her foot and stomped on Wesley's instep. Wesley yelped and released Lily just in time for Lily's mother to catch him across the face with a wicked slap. He staggered, his hands flying to his cheeks. When he pulled them away, they saw the big circles of rouge underneath, the blue eye shadow, the bright slash of lipstick.

"What? How?" Lily's mother hissed.

As Lily, her mother, Vaz, and Ms. Reedy stood, confused, paralyzed, they saw white, crosshatched lines etching themselves into his newly made-up skin. They deepened into depressions as he screamed.

Lily rubbed her neck where the gun had imprinted itself in the flesh. "What's happening to his face?"

"It's like he's caught in some kind of net," Ms. Reedy said. "I've never seen anything like it."

Wesley danced and twirled as the depressions became welts and his nose flattened and spread. He staggered around the grave-sized hole that had hidden the trunk, teetering on the edge. When he fell in, the rest heard the sickening snaps of breaking bones.

Vaz reached down and scooped up the gun. He peered over the edge of the hole.

"Is he dead?" Lily's mother said, grabbing Lily and giving her a fierce, protective hug.

A weak voice wafted up. *I'll get you, you filthy monkeys!*

"Guess not," said Lily.

"He won't be walking anytime soon," Vaz said. "It looks

like someone tried to tie his legs in a bow. And put on some lipstick. It's like the Makeover from Hell down there." He looked at Lily's mother and grinned, making a fist. "That's some right hook you got there."

"How did you untie yourself?" said Lily. "How did you know where we were?"

Lily's mother stared off into the distance. "I don't know," she said finally. "I felt something tugging at the ropes, and then they just . . . dropped off." She reached into her pocket. "I found this on the floor."

She held out a tarot card, a picture of a woman rising up from the ocean.

Vaz frowned at the card. "A naked woman?"

"The beach," said Lily's mother.

"Right," said Lily.

Bailey Burton stopped flailing and sat up, his piggy eyes finally focusing on Vaz, on the gun in his hand.

"Hey, Mr. Burton," Vaz said. "I didn't know you were such a great dancer. Any performances coming up? Need a manager?"

Bailey Burton panted and shivered. Someone had decorated his hair with little pink barrettes, and large pearl earrings dangled from his ears.

"We're going to open this trunk now. Any objections?" Vaz continued.

Burton curled his odd body around his huge head like an inchworm.

Lily dropped to her knees in front of the trunk and wrestled with the lock. All of a sudden it was the most important thing in the world. "Help me, Vaz."

"Somebody has to keep an eye on Burton, then."

"Let me watch my brother," Ms. Reedy said. She held out her hand for the gun.

"Are you kidding?" Vaz said.

"Give her the gun," said Lily.

Lily's mother looked doubtful. "Are you sure you trust her?"

Lily touched the bruise on Ms. Reedy's cheek. "We can try."

Ms. Reedy held the gun on her own brother while Lily and Vaz tried to open the rusted lock on the trunk. Vaz took a shovel and finally broke it.

"Okay," he said. "Your turn, Lily. Open it."

Lily pulled the shattered hasp from the latch and lifted the lid. Besides several large stones that had been used to give the trunk its weight, the only thing inside was a document, folded neatly in an unsealed envelope. Lily pulled out the papers and started to read.

"What is it, Lily?"

Lily smiled and held out the document for everyone to see. Along the top of the cream-colored sheets, in large calligraphic type, were these words:

The Last Will and Testament of
Katherine Spicer Wood.

Chapter 26

Katherine Wood had cut Wesley from her will and left everything she owned in the world to her daughter, Ruth, and Ruth's heirs, of whom only Lily and her mother survived.

They were not rich. Aurelia Reedy had been correct about Wesley's less-than-sharp business sense. Of the once huge estate with vast holdings in numerous business sectors, the house at 206 Perry Street was the only asset left. Lily's mother sold a bunch of antiques to pay the back taxes, and then she sold a bunch more to scrape together a deposit on Madame Durriken's Good Fortunes Shoppe, which she promptly renamed Trinket.

Vaz invited a bunch of his friends to help clean, paint, and decorate the new shop to turn it into a proper jewelry shop. These friends included Kami. To Lily's surprise, Kami seemed to think everything about Lily was cool, from her hair to her flea-market sneakers. Kami asked if she could have the now-famous Kewpie doll as a souvenir, but oddly, Lily couldn't find it anywhere.

Lily started school as planned and—just as Madame Durriken had predicted—soon found herself to be something she'd never been in her life: popular. Lily was smart enough to know that such things don't last but enjoyed it just the same, telling the story of the fire—and the murder—that had occurred more than forty years before. Everyone was fascinated by the arrest of insane Wesley Wood, hobbling from the courthouse in his double casts, and his henchman, Bailey Burton, and the crazy hunt for Captain Kidd's treasure. (The parents of many of these kids invested in metal detectors.)

Lily kept some things to herself. She didn't tell the other kids about the ghosts, of course. She didn't tell them how quiet the house was now, how Julep had taken to curling up in the kitchen sink rather than on top of the dining-room table. How she wished sometimes for the scent of smoke, of tea with mint.

Soon after the events on the beach, Lily sat at the dining-room table under the glittering chandelier. In her hand were her mother's pliers, the first time she had picked them up in years. She was trying to repair the chain that Wesley had broken when he'd ripped the coin from her neck. The work was harder than it looked.

She heard the door slam and her mother's footsteps in the hallway. Lily didn't look up. "How was your date?" she asked, trying not to appear too disgusted with the whole thing.

Her mother shrugged. "It was all right."

She was normally bubbling over with all kinds of plans after a first date. Lily stopped what she was doing. "Aren't you going out with him again?"

"I don't think so." Her mother made her kissy face, the face that usually meant she would say no more, but this time she did. "The guy went on and on about how wild and colorful and fascinating I am. After a while it was like he wasn't talking about me, he was describing some exotic bird from the Amazon."

Lily grinned. "My mom the toucan."

Her mother giggled. "Ha! You're the colorful one," she said, ruffling Lily's still-pink hair (she'd decided it was kind of cool and kept it, and it had started a mini-trend at school. She and Kami were planning on dyeing their hair blue in time for their freshman year.)

Her mother put her bag on the table. "What are you doing?"

"Trying to fix this chain. You could probably do it faster."

"You're doing fine. Pinch the link a little tighter and I think you've got it."

Lily angled for a better grip on the pliers. "I've been thinking," she said. "Wesley told the police that he'd hidden Katherine's will a million years ago, right? So how did it end up in the trunk? Katherine couldn't have buried it."

Her mother opened up her purse and began digging around inside. "Max probably buried it."

"That's what I thought. But he couldn't have buried it while he was alive, because she hadn't written it yet. It had to be after he died. When I was talking to him, he told me that he had made a deal with Captain Kidd, right? And the chest we dug up was really old, really, really old. You know what I think?"

"What?"

"That Max swapped the treasure for the will."

"If you say so."

"But if that's true, what happened to the treasure?"

Her mother put down her handbag and laughed. "You've grown quite an active imagination in the last month. I guess it was the bump on the head." She stretched.

Lily almost dropped the pliers. "Imagination? Wait a minute," she said, incredulous. "Are you saying that you don't believe there are ghosts?"

"Well, honey," her mother said, "I guess that the world would certainly be a much more interesting place if there were." She patted Lily's hand and walked, humming, into the kitchen.

Lily was so stunned that she told Vaz. "Even after Katherine untied and set her free! Even after Katherine left her the tarot card, she doesn't believe it! Even after what she saw at the beach."

"Maybe she *can't* believe it," Vaz said. "Not everybody can be as open-minded as you."

"Maybe," said Lily. She squeezed Vaz's hand, he squeezed back, and her heart squeezed in on itself.

When the glorious Cape May summer came, Lily and Vaz haunted the beach, collecting shells, playing Frisbee, riding the waves. At dusk they sat in the huge lifeguard chairs and thumb-wrestled between kisses, but mostly they left out the thumb-wrestling.

Lily also started dragging her mother to the water. Her mother soon adopted Diamond Beach, a stretch of sand where you could find tiny stones that could be cut and polished to look like diamonds. (Trinket soon became famous for its Diamond Beach Design line.) Lily and her mother wore it when they set up beach chairs in the living room to have picnics with the cat.

Sometimes, with the diamond ropes around her neck and the Indian rupee necklace in her fist, she curled up in her big bed, marveling at herself. Just a few months ago she wouldn't have believed they would find a place to stay awhile, maybe even forever. Too excited to sleep, she would turn on the light and flip open the new book her mother had given her, *To Kill a Mockingbird*. She had to admit that the book wasn't half bad (though not as cool as the microscope she was saving up for).

As exciting as Lily found her new life, she still liked to go to the beach alone. Watching the waves roll in, pull back, and roll in again caused a bittersweet ache inside her, the same ache she felt listening to Vaz's heartbeat, hearing Julep's odd quacking meow, watching her mother's intelligent hands twist wire into whimsy. Sometimes, when the tide went out, leaving only a shallow puddle to lap at the beach, Lily thought of her father. She knew that someday she would track him down and ask him why he had to go, why he'd chosen to become a ghost. But for today, her mother, Vaz, Kami, her cat, and the beach were enough.

e couple watched THE COUPLE WATCHED the couple watched THE COUPLE

The couple watched as the girl walked down to the water.

"She looks happy," said the man with the big belly.

"Yes, she does," said his wife. "But I wish she hadn't done that to her hair. It's awful."

"What's wrong with the hair?" the girl in fishnets said indignantly. "I like it!"

The wife harrumphed. "You would. And scoot over! You're hogging the whole sheet."

"Here's what I think," the girl said. "You guys heard of *Ghostbusters*, right? How about we make our own crime-fighting team, except we fight *living* criminals. Get it, ghosts who chase men instead of the other way around? I'm thinking of calling it *Manbusters*." She clapped her hands. "What do you think? Totally awesome, right?"

"Totally cracked," said the man.

"Cracked? Is that, like, good?"

The wife arranged the skirted bathing suit on her lap. "Don't you have something you need to do?"

The girl in the fishnets laughed. "Do? What's there to do *here*? Do! Ha! That's a funny one. That's . . . that's . . ." Suddenly she jumped to her feet, pointing at an extremely tall black woman in a lifeguard jacket. "That's *Steffie*! Omigod! It's her! I swear it is, on my mother's grave. Or on my mother's *future* grave, if she's not dead yet." She performed a few high kicks, spraying sand everywhere. "It looks like I've got something to do after all. See you guys later."

And she ran off, fuchsia skirt flapping.

The man gaped. "She's crazy as a bedbug."

"You sound surprised," his wife said dryly.

He met her eyes. "I'm surprised about you. You were something, you know. The way you went after those bad guys. There goes the bedsheet! Right over the head! They didn't even see you coming!"

"You were great, too," said his wife. "Who knew you were such a demon with sand toys? Loved the trick with the net." She patted the man's knee. "Don't look now, but there's your friend."

The man turned and squinted. "What friend?"

"Your pirate friend? The one with the sword and the feather in his hat?"

The man in the hat was reading off a yellowed piece of paper and counting to himself. "One hundred fourteen, one hundred fifteen, one hundred sixteen." He flung the paper aside, dropped to his knees in the sand, and began to dig.

"Will somebody please explain all the darned digging?" the man said.

"Shhh," said his wife.

The pirate dug and dug and dug. He reached into the hole he had made and hauled out a doll in a red dress. It had no head.

"What the heck?" said the man.

"Quiet," said his wife.

The pirate hefted the headless doll to his chest as if it were a very heavy child. Then he stood and began to walk toward the sea, passing right in front of the couple. A few silver coins with strange markings fell from the doll's neck and dropped to the sand, but the man didn't seem to notice. Soon he was up to his knees in the churning sea.

"Now I've seen everything," said the woman, floppy flowers flying. "I've seen all there is to see." She looked at the coin trail the man had left. "Should we pick them up?"

"Nah, leave 'em for the kids," said the man. He leaned toward his wife. "Listen, I've got an idea."

"I'm all ears," said the woman.

"What do you say we go find the car and call it a day?"

His wife smiled. "I thought you'd never ask."

Chapter 27

Lily strolled down the beach, inhaling the wonderful salty air. Out of habit, she scavenged for shells and used them to dig troughs in the cool, soft sand. She moistened the sand with ocean water she carried cupped in her hands, began another house with windows and a stone walk.

"Lily," a voice whispered.

She turned. It was near dusk, and the wide beach was empty.

Suddenly the house in front of her changed. As she watched, an invisible hand added a porch and a pebble driveway. Windows popped from the third floor. Red-and-purple stained Popsicle sticks flew through the air and stuck themselves into the sand to form a picket fence.

206 Perry Street.

Lily sat back on her heels, chills running up and down her spine, but pleasantly for once. "Hi, Max. You forgot the people. A house is just a house without the people."

She felt a tug in her chest and knew—though she couldn't have known, though the only sounds she heard were the cries of the gulls and the crash of the sea—that both Max and Katherine were there with her on the beach but were leaving for good. That it was time to say good-bye.

"Bye, Uncle Max," she said, her voice catching in her throat. "Bye, Grandma Katherine. Thank you."

She stood. The sense of loss was quickly replaced by a sense of fullness. She would see them soon enough.

She looked down at the beautiful sand house, but its perfection only made her yearn for the less-than-perfect real thing. She turned and ran up the beach, her feet fast and light. As she approached the promenade, she heard the words that made her turn one last time.

"Good-bye, Lily. Welcome home."